"Did you have a good time, Robby?" she asked, somewhat uncertain what his answer would be.

His eyes were closed and he was silent. Then he smiled. "Yes, Penny, I did. I don't know what came over me, but I did have a wonderful time."

"Do you feel guilty about it, Robby?"

"No. I guess not. Do you?"

"No. No." After a few moments of silence, she asked, "Do you want to sleep in bed with me tonight, Robby?"

He looked up into her eyes, and she kissed his nose. "I was going to ask you if I could, Penny. Can I?" he asked, his voice as innocent as his eyes.

"Yes, Robby. Yes. I want you to. I want you to stay with me tonight. I want to please you as you pleased me."

Other books by
MARY LOVE

Mastering Mary Sue
Wanda
Angela

VICE PARK PLACE

MARY LOVE

MASQUERADE BOOKS, INC.
801 SECOND AVENUE
NEW YORK, N.Y. 10017

First Masquerade Edition 1992

First printing February 1992

ISBN 1-56333-008-3

Cover Photograph © 1992 Robert Chouraqui
Cover Design by Eduardo Andino

Manufactured in the United States of America
Published by Masquerade Books, Inc.
801 Second Avenue
New York, N.Y. 10017

VICE PARK PLACE

Chapter One

Impressively fenced in and snobbishly private, Gramercy Park, New York, is filled, on any given temperate day, with imported nannies relaxing in the sun or shade, tending high, wide-wheeled baby carriages built in England and France. The impeccably cared-for shrubbery, lawns and towering trees are abundant. The park is, indeed, a special reservation. One needs a key to unlock the gate, and one must live on its north, south, east or west perimeter to be a member of the society of rich families who have exclusive use of the park's facilities.

When summertime ends and autumn appears with its cloak of many colors, the charm and magic of Gramercy Park increases with the lengthening shadows of the elaborate buildings and ornate last-century homes surrounding it. A veritable oasis in the center of the bustling city—Lexington Avenue pointing north like an arrowhead, Irving Place stretching to the south—Gramercy Park has the dimensions of a square city block. A tall, rugged statue of Washington Irving, the prolific writer, occupies a prominent place in the central plaza.

This is the locale of our little story, which just happens to be true.

A soft, late evening rain had just abated when Mrs. Penelope Luckner, age thirty, divorced, unusually attractive—even beautiful—and mother of eleven-year-old Jeffrey, glanced at the grandfather clock, impatiently waiting for it to strike the hour of ten. This solemn chime would signal her exit from the tall, rococo building in which she still lived in a large apartment awarded in the divorce settlement with Jeffrey's philandering, but nonetheless generous, father.

She had been married to George Luckner for eleven exhausting, sexually unsatisfying years. When

7

George was sober and industrious, he was a gem! But when he drank—and he was now a confirmed alcoholic—he was a first-class son-of-a-bitch. Mean and contemptible and jealous, he was physically threatening and psychologically brutal, punishing Penny for nonsensical misdemeanors and other trifling matters most husbands of George's rank would have easily tolerated as being part and parcel of the union of any two disparate individuals.

The legal separation and the subsequent divorce had been devoutly pursued by Penny, and the result of her efforts was an iron-clad agreement allowing visiting rights with Jeffrey and the like. The final settlement exceeded her wishes. Unfortunately, the reactive depression that overwhelmed her just days following the scene with the judge in his private chambers—the judge was an old family friend of George's—was as fearsome as a forbidding winter wind brutally knifing down a cavernous city thoroughfare.

After several sessions, emergency and otherwise, with a psychiatrist living in the same luxury building, Penelope politely severed her past from the present. She was determined to make new friends, determined to be a good mother to Jeff, and determined to occupy herself with every distraction she could find. After a few weeks of earnest yet dispassionate activity she had exhausted most of these resolutions, and was now in the habit of waiting until ten o'clock each evening and then leaving her comfortable but lonely apartment and strolling down Irving Place to the corner of Eighteenth Street. There she would sit at the bar in Pete's Tavern and drink three or four scotches. Sometimes she would exchange pleasantries with the amiable bartenders, or eat a shrimp cocktail at the bar. She firmly discouraged tavern prowlers, young and old alike, as she sat preoccupied and alone at the long, old-fashioned mahogany bar.

This particular evening the bar was nearly deserted. In the rear dining rooms the waiters talked quietly among themselves. Few people were dining out. There was an unseasonable chill outside; it was the Monday after the Labor Day weekend.

At the bar Penny removed her rainslicker and folded it neatly across her lap. Bob, the bartender, a cheerful smile on his round face, served her automatically. Saying nothing, he leaned back against the cash register. He appreciatively studied her appearance. Penny was wearing a tight cashmere sweater. He could see the firm, conical outline of her breasts swelling voluptuously under the expensive material. The twin points of her nipples were visible, and Bob noticed they were erect, seeming to poke lasciviously toward his eyes as she lit a cigarette and slipped it into her silver holder.

He saw that as usual she swallowed fully half of her drink and then fell into the pensive mood with which he identified her. He often wondered why such an attractive young woman as she had no escorts, but Mrs. Luckner, as he called her politely, kept her business to herself. He secretly admired her for this. She was quite unlike any of the other lonely women who sat at his bar.

The front door opened and in came someone who looked to be more of a boy than a man. But judging by the drink he ordered, a vodka on the rocks, he was most definitely not as young as he looked. Perhaps twenty, twenty-one at the oldest. When Penny saw his reflection in the mirror behind the bar, and then turned to look at him, she remarked to herself that he was probably too young to be drinking in a bar, but not too young to drink, which meant that he was probably closer to nineteen than to twenty-one.

"Dreary night," he said in a dull voice as he carried his drink to his full, red lips. Bob was about to agree with him when Penny turned to the young man and smiled. It was then that she saw how handsome he was.

"Yes, quite dreary," she said. Bob leaned back, folded his arms and smiled. He'd never seen Mrs. Luckner so suddenly animated before.

"Cheers," he said in a voice that was anything but cheerful. Penny lifted her glass into the air toward his. They both drank.

"Seems that the weather's got you down?" she asked, not quite knowing what had compelled her to say such an intrusive thing to a perfect stranger. "Here, let me buy you a drink." What had gotten into her? She fumbled in her purse for some money and handed it to Bob. "On me," she said, pointing to the boy with her glass.

The boy nodded in her direction, thanking her. He looked pensive as he watched the ice floating on the surface of his drink. His brow was furrowed, and he looked almost as if he would burst out crying at any moment.

"Is anything wrong?" Penny asked, curious. He seemed, indeed, to be held by the firm grip of some kind of depression. Perhaps it was only the weather. Perhaps it was none of her business. But she had already asked. She looked at him. His features were fine and his skin clean and flawless, unlike most of the late-night patrons of an empty bar. His hair, which was slightly tousled, was otherwise clean-cut. His body appeared strong, though she could not tell for certain as he was seated some stools away from her. But, all in all, his bearing was that of a man with incipient self-assurance. She liked men with certainty.

"No, not really," he answered as he took another sip from his drink. Penny had to think for a moment; she'd forgotten what she had asked. Oh yes, she had asked if any thing were the matter. The boy's appearance had overwhelmed her for a moment and she struggled to regain her composure.

"I had a fight with my old man," he said, and then brightening he added, "but it'll be okay, I guess. We always fight." The sincere hope that things would be okay was transmitted through his uplifted voice, and Penny laughed for some reason. Her laugh was like the sound of silver bells, and it caused both Bob and the boy to laugh, too, though no one was certain just what it was they were laughing at. But it felt good to Penny, for she hadn't laughed in a long, long time.

And then the boy grew pensive again, downing his drink and taking up the one Penny had bought for him. Again, Penny noticed his strong body and his full, sensual lips as they at to the edge of the glass. She imagined how it would feel to be kissed by them, and her loins stirred to the thought. It had been so long since she'd had such thoughts that the sensations stirring in her body made her uncomfortable. She shifted in her seat in order to diffuse them, but found that when she squeezed her legs together, the feelings surged with even greater intensity.

"The rich bastard said that I had to earn my keep, said I'm a freeloader, that I haven't done an honest day's work in my life." He looked at Penny. His eyes somehow imploring, as if he needed reassurance that he was anything but that which his father had called him.

"I'm sure that's not true," she said, responding only to his eyes. When she placed a cigarette between her lips, he leaned over and lit it for her. Her hands were cupped around the tip of it, in order to protect the flame from the air blowing from the tiny fan behind the bar, and his fingers brushed hers. She felt a small catch in her breath as she noticed how firm and strong his hands were. She saw then the insignia on his expensive ring. It bore the name of an important and quite prestigious boys' school, to which she'd considered sending Jeffrey when he became old enough. She said nothing about it though, as it would indeed make him too young to be drinking in a bar if he still went there.

As he leaned away from her, certain that her cigarette would burn on its own, he began speaking again. "My father said at dinner tonight that I was worthless. That I couldn't earn any money. That the money he gave me was a waste. He was angry as hell at something else, but he took it out on me! I know he did. He said that every one of his friends' sons had worked during the summer vacation and didn't loaf like me." He paused. "He's such a bastard, and I can tell you one thing: I'm not worthless!"

Penny smiled in recognition of his promise that he was not worthless. She could tell that some part of him doubted it, though. He smiled then, and Penny was impressed with his perfect, strong teeth. He had a beautiful smile.

"I'm sure you're not," she said soothingly. In a way, he reminded her of her son, though he was much older and very different. Perhaps it was simply a quality that all sons shared, one that made them unsure and yet certain of themselves at once—defiant and doubtful.

He drank the last of the second drink, extinguished his cigarette and thanked Penny. "I guess I'd better be getting back," he said hesitantly. He didn't really want to leave. But it was too risky. He'd already been served, that was true. But you never knew when the bartender was going to pull rank on you and ask for your ID. He didn't want to take the chance. It was too embarrassing getting kicked out of a bar for being a year underage. Anyway, he'd had enough. At his age, two drinks—two strong drinks—were almost enough to lay him flat out on his back. Tonight was different though, tonight he didn't feel so drunk. It was probably the fight, he thought soberly as he rose from his bar stool and thanked Penny again. Shaking her hand, his eyes lingered for a moment on the swell of her breasts. When her eyes caught his a slight smile crossed her face, and he felt ashamed. Almost apologizing, he hastily retreated.

When he was gone, Penny quickly finished her drink. She slipped her raincoat on.

"Leaving us early tonight, Mrs. Luckner?"

"Yes, I'm a bit weary, I must admit. Besides," she smiled graciously, "I've got to get home before it rains any harder. Dreary nights like these, it's best to be home with a book."

What she would have said, had she wanted to be completely blunt with Bob, was that she was aroused, that her cunt, that her panties had moistened as soon as she had realized the virile strength of the young man, sitting at the bar, that what she really wanted to do was far different than reading a book, that what she really wanted to do was follow the boy and take him to bed with her. But she wasn't completely blunt, and so instead she bade him good night and hurried out the door and up the street toward Gramercy Park. She was a half a block behind the boy and kept her eyes trained on his strong, quick strides. She had to walk fast in order not to lose sight of him.

Chapter Two

With Mrs. Luckner gone, Bob chuckled, and after methodically counting the night's take, he opened a newspaper to the racing page and checked. He had not won. Cleaning the bar, he saw Mrs. Luckner's silver cigarette holder lying near the dollar tip she usually left him. He wrote her name on a napkin and wrapped the expensive holder in it. From the cash register he took a rubber band and wrapped it securely around the small package. He placed it on the back bar. Strange, he mused, that she should be in such a hurry. Besides, she usually drank three or four more scotches.

In Gramercy Park, the wind was still gusting, showering raindrops from the leaves down onto the grass and the cement walks.

As Penny Luckner hurried along the wet sidewalk—her full, luscious breasts jiggling and swaying heavily from side to side, her long hair bouncing jauntily on her shoulders, her pussy alive as it hadn't in a long, long time—she spotted the boy reaching the dead end of Irving Place where the street abutted the fenced-in park.

She stopped when she saw him pause by the gate leading into the park. She saw him take a ring of keys from his pocket and, using one, enter through the gate. She watched, breathing quickly. He vanished into the very private solitude and darkness the park offered its privileged users.

Well, now! she thought to herself. Wasn't this something! Walking slowly, she rummaged in her purse for her own little-used key. Humming to herself and only half understanding what was driving her, she walked slowly in the direction of the huge gate. She stood under the streetlight, the light dancing on her long hair flushed outside the raincoat collar. She searched in her

15

purse for her cigarette holder, then remembered that she'd left it in the bar. She debated returning for it and then changed her mind. The wild sensations in her crotch were now radiating throughout her body, spreading up to her erect nipples. Experimentally, she reached inside the raincoat and cupped one breast, her fingers grazing over the stiffening nipple. She then looked in her purse for her compact. Finding it, she examined her makeup, her hair. Satisfied, she replaced the compact and lit a cigarette.

She felt a crazy fear stirring in her lower belly. What on earth was wrong? Why had this boy excited and aroused her so? It *must* be him, she mused, feeling a throbbing inside her pussy. Her swollen breasts ached. She realized her pussy was now dripping wet, and she felt a shade of embarrassment. Perhaps she should just go back to her apartment and read that book after all? But instead, she opened the gate and followed the boy, hoping, without actually knowing it on a conscious level, for a casual meeting.

Once inside the gate, she stood in the shadows. Turning her back to the statue of Irving and facing the street, shielded by large magnolia bushes, she reached her hand up under her skirt. *God!* she thought. *I'm soaking wet!* She hadn't been this excited since she was a teenager, on her first date with the man who two years later was to become her husband. She dismissed the thought and, raising her wet fingers to her nose, smelled them. She smiled. She smelled nice and clean, but the odor was distinctly that of desire.

Penny laughed at herself, her inner voice remarking that she'd been plenty stupid believing that she'd become frigid two years ago when George had stopped making love to her. Frigid? Anything but, judging from the warm, sexy sensations flooding her shivering body and the fragrant cream moistening her pussy and making damp the thin crotch of her panties. "Frigid, my ass!" she said aloud, and then let her skirt drop.

Humming to herself again, she started to circle the park. When she turned the corner at the north end, she saw the boy. He was sitting alone on a bench usually reserved for older citizens, where, in the daytime, a giant tree shaded the sun yet allowed its warmth to penetrate. In the deep, tree-shrouded shadows, she'd almost missed him. She saw the glow of a cigarette in his hand.

Holding her head high, and terribly conscious of her bouncing breasts and of her nipples rubbing against the soft material of her sweater, she walked past him, the raincoat wide open and flapping.

"Well, hello there!" his voice called out, and Penny Luckner's heart pounded.

She stopped tentatively and turned to face him. "Oh, it's you," she said, feigning surprise as best she could. "Are you allowed in here?" she asked.

"I have a key," he answered. "I guess you do too, huh?"

"Yes, I have a key. I seldom use it," she said, walking back toward him. "Only now and then."

"Me, I use mine a lot. I do my smoking in here. I'm not allowed to smoke in the house. One of the other things I'm not allowed to do."

"Your father sounds horrible."

"He is," said the boy. Then he moved over. "You can sit on the dry spot…if you want," he said matter-of-factly. "I don't care right now if I get soaked."

"Why…why, thank you," Penny muttered. Wasn't this all happening too fast? she thought, again feeling a distinct throb in her cunt, which made her long to touch him.

She sat down next to him. Their thighs brushed together momentarily and her spine began to tingle. The boy made no effort to move away, and she was terribly conscious of his nearness.

17

They exchanged names. "Mine's Robby," the boy said. "Robert F. Breining, if you want to be formal. My friends just call me Robby."

Penny told him her name, leaving off the "Mrs." They shook hands. "Glad to know you, Penny," he said, and the sound of her name from his lips thrilled her. Her heart pumped hard, and she could feel beads of perspiration forming in the deep cleavage of her ripe breasts. God, what was going on? she wondered as she listened to him explain where he lived and what subjects he liked best in school.

"Are you married?" he interrupted himself.

Penny began to lie, but changed her mind immediately. "I was, but I'm not any more. I'm divorced." Then, throwing all caution away, she told him about Jeffrey. She decided she might as well; she hated lying and insincerity. She told Robby that her young son had been away with his father for the summer, and would probably be away until the Christmas vacation, which he would spend with her here in the city, at Gramercy Park. He would then return to his father until the completion of the school year, when he would come back to live with her for the following year.

"I wish I had that kind of arrangement. I have to stay with my father all of the time. And he's such a tyrant, he is. I don't like him at all, either as a father or as a man."

Penny pondered this. She'd scarcely been listening, so preoccupied was she with his closeness, the feel of his strong thighs against hers, the odor of his hair tonic and the deep resonance of his voice. She alighted to his words, though, when he began to tell her how old he was.

"I'm a senior in high school, or I will be as soon as school starts anyway, but I'm eighteen. This, you see, is part of the problem my father has with me, and yet it's his fault. When I was a kid my parents traveled a lot, and usually they took me with them. When I was five they took me to England with them. We stayed for a year. They didn't want to start me off in a school there, so they kept me out a year, and I started when I got back, a year behind everyone else. My father doesn't seem to remember this, and thinks that because I'm eighteen, I should be getting ready to go to college and earning money for it at the same time."

Penny thought about this. Eighteen wasn't so young; it wasn't as young as fifteen or sixteen anyway. It was that he was still in high school that made him seem as young as he did. He seemed, in fact, quite innocent, quite inexperienced, which she guessed he probably was. But still he was eighteen; eighteen to her thirty. There was quite a difference she thought, laughing to herself. Even thinking about it made her loins stir. She'd hadn't ever thought of herself as someone who preferred younger men. That thought made her laugh aloud.

"What are you laughing at?" he asked. "You laughing at me?" He lit another cigarette and then offered one to her. She took it, and he asked about her cigarette holder.

"I do miss it," she said softly, trying to keep from shivering, "but I'll pick it up tomorrow sometime, I guess." He offered to run back and get it for her right then, but she reached out and held his wrist, telling him he was not to bother. The touch of his flesh against her hand sent fire through her fingers.

Her heart was thumping. "Do you have a girl-friend?" Penny asked, trying to keep her nervousness from her quavering voice. Christ, she was beginning to feel like a young, silly virgin with her first serious boyfriend.

"Nope. Can't stand girls my own age. They bore me. Always giggling, carrying on. I don't get along with them."

"You like older girls?" How did she dare ask?

"Oh, a little, I guess. I'm not really experienced at all," he went on seriously, honestly. "I'm still a virgin."

"Well, I guess so, if you don't like any girls your own age."

"Most of my pals aren't virgins anymore, and they're all younger than me! Funny, isn't it? The girls seem to like experienced guys better, too. Unless they really like you, they don't give you a second thought. I keep mostly to myself."

Penny felt a tremendous pulsing in her loins. Everything about him made her want him; she wanted to run her hands all over his strong, youthful body; she wanted to kiss his full mouth, to taste him. "Well, there's plenty of time, I suppose."

"Yes, I suppose there is, Penny," he said, a kind of resignation in his voice.

"Well, don't sound so sad."

"I'm not sad."

"You sounded a bit sad."

"No. Hell no. I'm not sad about that. I can wait. To tell the truth, girls don't even excite me. I'm beginning to think there's something wrong with me, Penny, really. Maybe I'm sterile or something, huh?"

Oh, seduction! Penny was thinking now. How do they do it?

"Do you confide in everyone, strangers, like this, Robby?" she asked. Truthfully, she was beginning to feel a weird empathy for the boy. They were talking together like friends of equal age, with no disparity between them.

"No. But to tell the truth, I feel kind of comfortable sitting alone here with you, smoking like this. I liked that you didn't warn me about cancer or anything like that. I feel kind of good with you. Usually I'm scared of older women, but not with you."

"That's a sweet compliment, Robby," Penny said, and then she lapsed into silence, her mind racing. Should she leave now that her cigarette was finished, have another, plan to meet him at the bar tomorrow evening? What should she do? She was stymied.

"Don't you have to be home at a certain time, Robby? It's getting late." The church chimes in the near distance tolled the hour of eleven.

"No. The old man's away for a week. He flew off just after he told me what a good-for-nothing leech I was. He'll be back Friday night. That's not unusual. But what pisses me off, excuse me, is that he was so mad that he didn't leave me any allowance, told me to go out and earn my spending money. Everything else's provided for, you see. Fridge full and that large apartment all to myself. No dog to walk, no cat to feed, just me and that damned empty apartment. I'm already sick of reruns, and the news doesn't interest me."

"What about reading?" she offered helpfully. She turned and faced him, her eyes caressing his handsome face. She loved his deep brown eyes, his perfect nose, and especially his sensual mouth.

"I get enough of that in school. I like it, but I'm too nervous now to read."

"How about games, sports, that sort of thing?" She felt her body melting now. The aching in her cunt was almost unbearable. She felt as if her breasts were going to burst if they weren't touched soon.

"Naw, maybe Monopoly or something like that. I'm not much for sports. I'm going to be a scientist like my old man, and sports takes up too much time. But I do like Monopoly; I don't know just why. That's funny, huh?"

Penny laughed. "I like it, too." This was true. She had played hundreds of games with Jeffrey before he went off with his father.

"We could play sometime," she said. "Have a set?"

"No. Sorry, I don't." He smiled at her, and she could have fallen into his mouth. When he licked his lips with the tip of his tongue, she became completely rattled, wild shivers shooting all over her body. She considered at least touching his leg, his arm, something harmless like that. She kept swallowing uncontrollably, her voice caught in her throat.

"Well...well, Robby," she said slowly, spacing each word to guarantee that it would issue from her trembling lips, "I have a set. It's kind of used. The money's not crisp, but..."

"When do you want to play, Penny?" he asked enthusiastically.

"Is it too late for a game tonight?" How she managed to blurt this out, she'd never understand. A bolt from the heavens, she thought, from the gods that hover over lonely divorcees sitting on private park benches with good-looking eighteen-year-old boys with strong, magnificent bodies, must have zapped down and singled her out for the strike.

He stood up. He took her hands and pulled her up. "Hell, no. Let's go. You said you had a set at home, right?"

"Right," she said, sounding more certain than she felt.

"Well, let's go then, okay?"

"But don't you think it's a bit late?"

"Not for me, if it's not for you!"

Her knees were shaking. "It's not too late, Robby," she said, and led the way out of the park to the building in which she lived.

Chapter Three

At the entrance to her building, the reality of what she was doing, of what she was about to do, struck her. What would Charlie the doorman think when he saw her entering at this hour in the company of a young man? There was no question that Robby looked quite young, his strong, masculine body notwithstanding. But she need not have worried because they entered the self-service elevator and climbed to the top floor unseen. Penny was deep in her own thoughts while Robby began to analyze the situation for the first time.

"Here we are," said Penny, smiling through her teeth, unable to suppress a feeling of silly helplessness. It was as if she were happily leading the way to her own execution. "Down this hallway. It's not too far," she heard her voice explain. Why was her tone apologetic? Why?

The overwhelming arousal she had experienced in the park now seemed to be curdling in her stomach. A creeping fear was replacing it. A fear of being caught? A fear that Robby might reject her? It was definitely a fear, but she couldn't define it.

Once inside her apartment Robby followed her into the luxurious living room, and she felt more safe, surrounded as she was by her own things. She turned on the lamp by the couch. Then she crossed the wide, carpeted room to the chest. Robby stood watching her. She leaned over to open it. In this position, her buttocks were round and full, perfectly formed. From them stemmed her long legs, the muscles in them lengthening so that it seemed her legs stretched far beyond her to the ceiling. She reached into the chest, displaced a few other games and withdrew with the Monopoly set. She turned then to face him. He looked somewhat bewildered she thought, and she straightened her skirt over her legs.

"Here it is, Robby," she said. "Be a dear and set it up for us. I have to use the bathroom." She moved toward him and he took the game from her hands. Their fingers brushed. He thought her hand had lingered on his for somewhat longer than was necessary, but he couldn't be sure. He looked to her eyes for the answer, but they were dark and mysterious, and from them he gleaned nothing, except perhaps an instinctive understanding of her desire. But as it was only instinctive he could not define it, and so he looked away from her, utterly confused. She surveyed him unnoticed. He was an inch or two shorter than she, not yet fully grown. They had similar noses. He was beautiful.

"Excuse me," she said. He looked after her as she walked down the hall to the bathroom. Her walk was fluid, sensual. He felt his cock stirring in his trousers, and he looked around the room in order to abate whatever it was that was stirring in him. He was impressed with her apartment. It was, in fact, quite magnificent. The windows were tall and stretched the whole expanse of the far wall. Everything was clean, spotless really, and in the corners there were huge ceramic pots, in which grew small tropical trees. There were freshly cut flowers all over the place. One wall contained nothing but books. Robby doubted he'd read any of them, but was impressed nevertheless. He moved to the fireplace and looked at a photograph of Penny's son on the mantle. Nice-looking kid, he thought. He looked like his mother.

And then he thought about how exactly the boy's mother did look, and again his cock stirred. She really was beautiful. And she had to be twenty years older than him, at least! At his age, everyone seemed ancient. But there was something ageless about her, something incredibly sexy about her, far sexier and more youthful, in fact, than the girls his age.

In the bathroom, Penny stepped out of her panties

and threw them onto the wicker hamper opposite the toilet. Bending over, she unlaced her new boots and took them off, too. Now she was barefoot, and the tile floor was cold but soothing to the soles of her feet. She wanted to undress completely, for she felt constrained in her clothes, but she knew that was impossible. The boy would be scared out of his mind if she were to walk into the living room naked. She laughed to herself, thinking about the expression that would fall over his face were she to emerge from the bathroom without any clothes on.

She went to the mirror and looked at her reflection, picking up a brush and running it through her hair as she did. She pouted her lips to see what they would look like to Robby were she to kiss him. Again she laughed, this time at how silly she was being. He was just a boy. She was a grown woman, and yet she was acting younger than him. Examining herself, she realized that there really was no need to be so unsure, so nervous about the whole thing. She was a beautiful woman, and he was just a young kid. He was probably completely enraptured with her, which would, she thought, explain his look of bewilderment. But on the other hand, he could be so innocent as to never suspect a thing about what was going on in her experienced mind. She shouldn't have brushed her fingers over his wrist, she thought.

Turning away from the mirror, pleased with what she had seen in it, she went to get a new pair of panties. And then she stopped. Why should I? she thought. And the idea of being pantiless beneath her short skirt thrilled her. Yes, that'll be something, she thought. I'll sit on the couch carelessly, so that my skirt hitches up to my waist, or I'll bend over so that he can see the bottom curves of my ass. Her body ached to think about it, and she ran her hands under her sweater and fondled her breasts. I'll spread my legs ever so slightly, she thought, pinching her erect nipples hard between her forefinger and thumb, and he'll not be able to help glimpsing my hungry cunt.

She turned back to the mirror and lifted her sweater. The swell of her breasts was perhaps the most alluring thing about her. It was perfect, really, the way they swelled like white, flawless, converging hills. And her nipples were the color of rose, deep rose when hard. They were large and stood out a good distance from her flesh. How that would arouse him, she thought, to catch a glimpse of my breasts. She lowered her sweater and unbuttoned the top three buttons so that the deep line of her cleavage could be seen, and the swelling curves of her breasts imagined.

"It's all ready, Penny," he said, seeing her walking down the hallway. As she came into the room, he could see the lissome movement of her breasts beneath the soft fabric of her sweater. "God, you're gorgeous," he said, not knowing exactly what he was saying yet feeling a need to say something, to speak instead of stare.

"Thank you, Robby." She shook her head and her long hair bounced luxuriantly on her shoulders. She saw his eyes dart to the milky white flesh revealed by the open sweater. She was extremely conscious of the sensual motions of her large breasts, and of her protruding nipples, which seemed to be growing stiffer although the pain had diminished slightly.

Passing by him, she paused. "I'm going to get some sherry. You drink wine, Robby?"

"I'll drink poison!"

Penny laughed. In the modern, gleaming kitchen, which Clara, the maid who came each day, kept sparkling, she produced an expensive bottle of imported sherry. She placed it along with two wine glasses and a corkscrew on a tray. Deciding all was ready, she paused. She lifted up her skirt to touch herself briefly before returning to Robby. Her desire was such that it was painful to leave it unattended for longer than a few minutes. The folds of her cunt were damp, spotted with the dew drops of her desire. She rubbed it into her flesh, lightly brushing her hand over her clitoris, which thundered in response to the touch. She was compelled by the rush of sensations to keep touching it. She circled her finger around and around it, on the verge, she was certain, of collapsing on the floor in utter weakness. But she had already been gone too long. She withdrew her finger, pulled her skirt back down her legs and, before picking up the tray to return to Robby, smelled her finger. It was fragrant, like wild flowers, she thought. He would surely be made drunk by that, if not the wine. Then, into the living room she went, still trembling slightly, but brave.

She placed the tray on the long coffee table facing the wide, leather couch. This coffee table, Robby had noted, was the longest and widest he'd ever seen. Sitting in the center of it, the Monopoly set looked lost. Each of the four table legs was buried in a round, ball-shaped glass caster, and he was surprised how easily and effortlessly the table could be moved. He laughed. With an air mattress on it, someone could use it as a bed, that's how wide and long it was.

"What Jeff and I usually do when we play, Robby, is this." She pressed a button and the long, leather couch became sectional, the ends moving around and shortening the space existing between the people who sat there. Two massive, leather cushions now made backrests. The extra pillow in the center of the couch formed a table.

"That's neat!" Robby exclaimed. "Really!" He'd never seen such a contraption.

"It cost a lot," Penny admitted, "but it's worth it. See, you can lie down, sit up, stretch out, and if you need to put your feet on the floor, you just slip around and do it."

As Penny demonstrated the use of the couch in

this new position, her short skirt flying up, her breasts jiggling under her open sweater, Robby's heart started pounding. He felt a gnawing sensation in his penis, a strange flood of excitement which was vaguely familiar to him from forbidden masturbation. He was sure he'd caught a glimpse of her dark pussy, and he loved her swollen breasts. How he longed to cup them in his hands! When she leaned forward to place one of the black leather cushions against the backrest, one of her breasts almost leaped out of the sweater. He caught his breath. Then when she bent over to lift up the Monopoly set and place it in the center of the couch, he saw the unmistakable curve of her naked buttocks. There was no doubt of it! He thought that if she were wearing panties, they must be very brief and very black. Thrill after thrill surged over him, causing him to swallow deeply and blink his eyes.

While Robby counted out the play money, referring to the instructions printed on the inside of the box lid, Penny opened the wine. Wordlessly, Robby reached over and poured a sample into his glass, and then, testing it, smiled and professionally, adult-like, filled her glass and then his own. She raised her sherry in a toast.

"Robby, I believe we're going to be friends, so here's to us, to our new friendship!"

"You are very kind," he said softly, and he meant it. He couldn't remember any adult treating him this way. He felt extremely at ease with her. He liked her. He liked how she smelled, how she dressed, how she laughed. She had giggled once and he liked this too. He liked the way she offered him a cigarette from the Chinese box on the end table; the way she handed him the lighter to light hers first and then his own.

"Okay if I kick off my shoes?"

"By all means," Penny answered, squirming around on the couch, wine glass in one hand, cigarette in the other. "Kick off whatever you want." She blushed slightly and tucked her legs under herself, conscious that all he had to do was lower his eyes a moment, and any doubt he might have about panties or no panties would be erased.

Behaving as casually as possible, she shook the dice to determine who would go first. She heard him sigh, and her eyes darted to his crotch. She could have sworn she saw his cock throb. Pretending to stare at the board, checking her supply of paper money, she saw the outline of his prick lengthening. She clearly saw the head enlarging. She saw him shift his buttocks, and when she raised her eyes to his she saw him staring up her flared skirt, his tongue wetting the corners of his mouth and his deep, dark eyes riveted to her shadowy, mossy nest, which was so casually and naturally displayed for his gratification.

During the first fifteen minutes of the game, Penny's restlessness increased. So did Robby's. He was constantly shifting his position, legs out, feet on the floor, legs crossed, up on his knees, and finally leaning back with his stockinged feet on either side of the playing board. She could see that his cock was rock-hard now, urged firmly against his belly under the constraints of his trousers, almost reaching to his belt, round and thick and long. How the sight of it excited her!

Several times she pretended to fix her skirt, but then she'd move soon after, either to flick her cigarette ash into the ashtray at the far side of the table, or to reach for the wine glass, and her skirt would slide back up her milky white thighs. Each time this happened, she was acutely aware of his eyes following the path of her skirt, marveling at the perfection of her legs. Her pulse beat rapidly, her blood threatening, it seemed, to explode from her veins. How long could this go on? She didn't think she could stand much more of it, this teasing, this waiting. She wanted him now.

When he wasn't looking, she looked at his lap. It was bulging, there was no doubt about it. The outline of his cock could be clearly seen, the magnificent dimensions of it expanding even more, screaming to be freed from his trousers. She longed to run her fingers up and down the length of it, to feel the hardness of it pressing into her palm. She longed to please him as she knew he had never been pleased before. She could lean down right now, if she wanted to, and wrap her lips around it, slowly slipping it from his trousers as she pressed her mouth hard against it. She could do that if she wanted to. She could also lean over and kiss his full, sensual lips. And then she could take his cock into her hand, her mouth, her cunt.

His hand moved to cover himself. He was extremely self-conscious of his erection, having never had one so close to a woman before, and he shifted his position in an attempt to hide it. He felt as if he'd been drugged, so overwhelming were the strange sensations that flooded his body. He was certain that she was aware of how he felt. It embarrassed him a great deal. He had to clear his throat before he could speak.

"Penny...Penny, could I ask you to close your eyes for a second, huh? I have to get up and go to the bathroom."

"Well, why should I close my eyes, Robby?" she asked innocently.

"Oh, don't ask me. Because...just because," he said, seeming both embarrassed and annoyed that she should ask in so soothing and so sexy a voice.

"I'll close my eyes, Robby, if that's what you want."

He knew she understood. How could he get up with his immense erection sticking out so obscenely?

30

He had fought to keep it down, thinking of the most unappealing things, anything to get his prick back to normal. But it hadn't worked.

When he got off the couch, his leg accidentally knocked down a row of fragile plastic houses and one hotel. He was exceedingly nervous. "Geez, I'm sorry, Penny!" he exclaimed. With his back toward her, he stood and walked awkwardly in the direction of the bathroom.

Chapter Four

When Penny heard the bathroom door close and the toilet seat being lifted up, hitting the porcelain tank, she raised up her skirt so that her bare buttocks and her flaming pussy touched the refreshing coolness of the leather cushion. Crossing her legs Indian-style, she cupped her pussy lovingly, rubbing the palm of her hand against the tingling lips, feeling the frothy juices wet her hand. She maneuvered two fingers inside and wiggled the tips of them, feeling the moist inner walls sucking them further in. She moved her fingers rapidly, her head thrown back, her eyes flickering in the immense pleasure. This, coupled with the memory of exposing her slit, and the sight of the boy's throbbing prick through his trousers, made her pussy melt with wanton lust.

With her other hand, she tantalized her erect clitoris. She thumbed and fingered it. She pinched it lightly and convulsed as the fiery bud began to expand, sending warmth rushing through her body, which trembled under the immense burden of her desire. Her full, round breasts ached from the delightful anguish she was suffering, and she imagined the boy in bed, the boy naked on the floor in front of her, his lips and his mouth making love to her pounding cunt. She imagined his cock, swaying stiffly before him as he attended to her needs.

Her fingers raced in and out of her expanded cunt, dancing wildly around her hardened clitoris and then lingering there, softly brushing over it. She moaned and felt the blood rushing to her head, making her feel weak. Her thighs ached from the strain of holding them open as she jostled her fingers, inserting yet another, now three, into her dark, seemingly endless passageway.

33

Again the movements of her her fingers grew calm, languorous. With the relaxed ease of one who had all the time in the world, she gently massaged herself, letting her thoughts drift, though she kept an ear cocked for the sound of the bathroom door opening.

It would not open anytime soon though, because, once hidden away in the bathroom, Robby took the opportunity to ease himself of the tremendous agony of his erection. He had to! He couldn't just sit there next to Penny with an obvious erection.

Dropping his pants, he sat on the toilet. His cock stood out straight and hard in his lap. Slowly, he closed his fingers around it, squeezing it hard. His palm lay against the hot flesh, and he began to work it up and down. It was then that he noticed her panties on the hamper. With some effort, he took his hand away from himself and walked over to pick up her panties. He smelled them, he kissed them, even sticking out his tongue to taste them.

He sat back down and draped them over his hand. Again, he wrapped his hand, now ensheathed with Penny's panties, around his cock. The material was slippery and at first cold. Soon, though, it was warmed by the heat from his flesh, and the feeling became exquisite. It did not take long for his pleasure to reach the exploding point. The very idea that he was masturbating with an older woman's panties was enough to make him come. He rubbed hard, the slippery material slipping up and down the length of him, and shuddered uncontrollably. His mind went black, his body overcome by pleasure, and he forgot to pull the panties away at the last minute. Instead, he came onto them, wetting them thickly with his release. Panicking, he put the panties back on the hamper, careful to hide the part of them, the crotch, into which he'd come.

Still touching herself, Penny's thoughts had taken

her to her husband. More than two years had passed since she'd had proper intercourse, a good fuck. Two stupid, fallow years with George, who never had the time. Always too tired, always too drunk and unable to admit it. And if she tried to play with herself and he discovered it, she'd suffer a ferocious verbal assault from her husband, invariably followed by half-hearted attempts on his part to reconcile his lack of attention or to rationalize it, faulty excuses that became so monotonous she could almost anticipate his every word.

Desperate, she had tried an affair with one of George's business acquaintances, but this had been a complete fiasco. George had found out and the punishment he had inflicted on her had been terrifying. He had even blackened her eye, knocking her to the floor of the family room in the house they'd rented on Long Island that summer.

She had left him maybe eleven times during the marriage, disgusted, listless, and then electrified by the hope of a reconciliation which lasted only as long as her husband remained sober. One martini and the reconciliation was invariably blown to smithereens.

Where was the tenderness she yearned for, the love, the deep, abiding affection she'd contracted for in the marriage everyone thought was made in heaven? Oh, if they only knew! If they only knew the true facts! She was a woman deprived of that which she most treasured, that which made her feel alive: intimacy. And it seemed to her especially cruel because she was remarkably pretty, with an excellent figure—large, voluptuous breasts with perfect nipples; a soft, but firm, belly; and an exuberantly healthy body.

But it was starving. She took excellent care of it, but it was starving. She dressed it in expensive garments, always in the height of fashion, always sexy, but moderate, sometimes almost indecent, but always this side of being obscene or vulgar. Yes, her body was starving, hungry for love, but she had no hope. She had nothing other than Jeff's coming home at Christmas to look forward to. And she had nowhere to go. The few people whom she did know were going their own ways, into their own chaos of separation and eventual divorce, hoping for happiness, which seldom, if ever, smiled upon them, just as it had failed until tonight to smile upon her.

She heard the bathroom door open and quickly she sat up properly, her skirt still high, exposing the length of her thighs but hiding the nexus of them. She shifted, pulling the skirt a safer distance down her legs and furtively felt her clitoris through the fabric of her skirt. As Robby approached her, smiling, she gave her clitoris one last pinch, moaned quietly and smiled at him tenderly.

"What was all that about, the moaning, Penny? Were you humming your favorite funeral dirge?" He was completely recovered, she saw, and somehow seemed more certain of himself than he had been before. She wondered if he had jerked off in the toilet.

"No, I was just moaning, thinking about how you might beat me at this game, Robby. You know you're way ahead already. I put back the houses."

"I see," he responded, helping himself to another glass of sherry. He looked at her seriously. "I don't feel like playing anymore right now, Penny. Do you feel like talking? I do."

"Sure, Robby. Let's talk."

"This wine's making me warm; do you mind if I take off my shirt, or just open it?"

She caught her breath. She hadn't anticipated this. She felt a violent surging in her pussy as she let her fingertip graze over her clitoris. "Sure...oh sure...take it off altogether, if you like. I don't mind. I'm used to boys without their shirts on."

"And I guess without their pants on too, huh?" he joked.

"I guess so...without their pants on too," she repeated, a withering thrill cascading from her brain to the tips of her naked toes.

"But I'll keep on my pants, okay?" There was a definite change in the tone of his voice. He sounded more superior, more sure of himself, she thought. Maybe even a little cocky.

"Okay, Robby, keep your pants on." Then she laughed. She guessed what he meant. Her panties! Of course! He had seen them on the wicker hamper in the bathroom. He had probably examined them, touched them. The thought excited her and she closed her eyes momentarily, the image of it over-whelming her.

"You're teasing me because you know I don't have any panties on, right?" As she spoke, she opened her eyes slowly.

He flushed. This was the first time she had seen the blood race to his face. He looked away. He was definitely embarrassed. He kept his eyes averted as he unbuttoned his shirt and slipped out of it. He fold-ed it neatly and placed it on the back of the couch.

"Maybe so," he answered, clearing his throat. "Maybe so." He was suddenly silent. He drank almost half of the wine and reached for the bottle. Gripping it firmly, he filled her glass again and then his own.

He raised his glass. His eyes were gleaming, but she could tell he had strong control of his emo-tions.

"Here's to the South of France where the girls don't wear no pants!" He laughed and drank the entire glass of wine in one huge gulp.

"Robby! Robby, you shouldn't drink so fast. You'll get drunk, or tipsy at the very least, and then what will I do with you?"

He pretended to be drunk, which amused her. He was very funny and convincing, weaving his body and making gibberish sounds as he raised and lowered one hand and fumbled on purpose for the bottle.

"Then," he said, slurring his words, smiling, wobbling his head, "then you'll have to undress me and put me to bed."

"Oh, Robby, you're funny," she said, laughing at his exaggerated, drunken mannerisms. But his meaning was clear. And so, apparently, was hers.

"Do you like drunks, Penny?" he asked, giggling. He carefully lifted the Monopoly board and placed it on the coffee table. Then he took the cushion and put it on the floor next to the couch.

"I adore them, especially when they're young like you."

"I'm not so young," he said soberly. "I'm a big boy now and I'm going to be bigger yet, get married, have brats, make lots of money, play around with blondes in bikinis, play the market like my father, be a high-paid scientist, and fly to the moon and die up there all alone. How's that, Penny?"

"I like everything except the part about dying alone on the moon." She swallowed her wine and he followed suit. This time she refilled the glasses.

Robby slipped off the couch and sat on the cushion on the floor, close to her bare feet. "I like you, Penny," he sighed. "I like you without your panties on. Do you think you'd like me without my pants?"

"Yes. Yes, I do, Robby. I think I would like you... very much." Her voice sounded so serious, even to herself, that she felt somewhat confused. The quickening in her pussy became much, much more intense than it had been. She was breathing with short, rasping breaths as he looked up at her. He reached for her bare toes and began to touch and caress them. A profound silence settled in the huge room. Penny could hear the loud ticking of the grandfather clock in the foyer. The last time she'd heard it toll, the hour was twelve-thirty.

He was tickling her toes now. Tenderly, he bent his head and brushed his lips across them.

"Oh, my toes aren't clean, Robby. Don't do that."

"They're clean enough for me, Penny," he said softly, and Penny could suddenly visualize him as a lover sitting at her naked feet, stroking her ankles as he was doing now, his fingers caressing and fondling her toes.

"Would you die on the moon with me, Penny?" His deep brown eyes were boring into hers. She felt her body trembling as his fingers climbed higher up her leg, to her knees now, massaging and squeezing, his fingertips teasing and tickling her flesh.

"Yes, I would, Robby. I would."

She would never be able to explain her next movement. A terrifying tenderness welled up in her. She felt her eyes moistening, her heart skipping beats. She reached for his head with both hands. He inched closer to her. His hands were now above her knees, kneading the warm, milky white flesh of her lower thighs. She could feel the folds of her cunt opening, her milky cream moistening them as he let his fingers climb higher and higher.

She drew his head closer. She bent over and kissed his hair, and deeply inhaled the smell of it. Then, turning his head gently, she kissed his ears, wetting them with the tip of her delicate, pink tongue. His body coursed with shivers. Finally, she bent her head back and kissed him fully on the mouth. She felt the tip of his tongue against her open lips, the warmth of his breath, the aroma of the sherry, the wetness of his tongue as it slowly, very slowly, slipped between her lips and touched her own tongue. They pressed their mouths gently to one another, hardly moving, each enjoying fully the soft pressure of the other's lips.

"Oh, Robby!" she sighed. "Where are we going?

What are we doing?" As she spoke, her humid breath moistened the fine hairs on his face.

"We're going to the moon to die together," he said.

"Oh, Robby! Robby! My little darling." She was crying now, wet tears dribbling down her cheeks, her body shivering as she felt his fingers slowly but inevitably advancing up her legs. His touch, though not expert, was certain, and his fingers worked their way toward her cunt with a determination born of inexperience found only in the young. She spread her legs slightly to make it easier for him to find his way. She was certain he had never touched a woman's cunt before. And then, without warning, his finger brushed against her outer folds. Her body convulsed, for nothing was, to Penny, so powerful as that first touch. He slid his finger then along the length of her folds, displacing them and moving to the center of her cunt, where it opened flower-like to let him in.

She kissed his head, his face, her tongue slashing and swirling in and out of his mouth, colliding with his own. And then, lowering his head, he slowly parted her warm thighs with his hands, his fingers sinking into the tender flesh. She let him raise her skirt and helped him by lifting her buttocks off the couch. He looked up into her eyes. His were solemn, serious. He looked unreal, dream-like to her.

He placed his lips on her soft flesh, licking it as he did. She shuddered. His mouth swept over her inner thighs, his lips parted slightly so that he traced a line of moistness with his tongue and humid breath. And then his mouth was at the entrance of her cunt. She threw her head back, feeling his hot breath on her wetted flesh.

Then she felt the tip of his tongue come out to lightly touch her smoldering mound. A powerful tension overtook her weakened body, and she arched her back on the couch to have his tongue more fully upon her. With his tongue, he moved the damp hairs aside, exposing the glistening inner lips of her pouting cunt. "Oh, Robby!" she gasped, as he sank his tongue into her marvelous, perfumed wetness.

Chapter Five

As though seized by the Devil himself, she writhed on the leather couch, unmindful of the fact that her flesh stuck painfully to it in her heated desire. Her skin could have been torn from her body for all she cared just then. She moaned as his mouth came heavily onto her cunt. He pressed it there, his tongue extending and, having no place else to go, driving into her passage. He twisted it inside her, causing her, by extension it seemed, to likewise twist on the couch.

And then he withdrew his head, and using his fingers, he spread the lips of her cunt wide and gazed upon her. Her cunt was far more beautiful than he'd ever imagined one being, and he'd spent long hours imagining just that. It was pink and red and circular, endlessly circular so that it seemed to open away from itself, while at the same time curving into itself like a flower. And the taste of it! It was sweet and salty and thickly fragrant. The wetness of it was like honey and he leaned down to it to taste her again. He was intoxicated with her nectar.

He lapped at her, wanting to be nourished by her, to drink from her that which would keep him alive, and yet he did not know what it was. He did not know that some women flowed with a similar substance as men when they came. He did not know that he was making her come just then. But as he worked his tongue around and around the outline of her cunt, darting it into her and pulling it out to circle it around her clitoris, which he had seen was dark and erect, quick spasms rushed through her body, making her cunt expand and contract around his tongue. She heaved forward and her wetness flowed into his mouth, glazing his lips, coating his tongue.

Not knowing that he had made her come, Robby

did not pull his head away when the strange pulsing motions of her cunt ceased. Instead, he licked up the creamy liquid which flowed from her, spreading it over his lips as he did, and continued to work his tongue in and out of her. She was delirious, and almost in pain. When his tongue came out to touch her clitoris, it was indeed painful, and she squirmed away. But how good it felt to have it buried deep within her. He spread her juices over the sensitive flesh, soothing her as if it were balm and his tongue the gentlest of fingers.

When he withdrew to breathe for a moment, she looked at him. His face was smeared with her release. He looked so young then, and so enthralled with his new knowledge. She smiled at him and he smiled back, raising up to kiss her. His mouth came down over hers, and she tasted herself, licking his lips, his chin, his cheeks. They laughed, and he returned to the warm comfort of her thighs.

How she longed to fuck him. But that could wait, she thought. She would wait until he was ready. Just now, he seemed too intent on learning every intricate crevice of her cunt. And she would let him. She would let him learn her entire body at as slow a pace as he desired. It felt too good to be attended to in this way. No one had ever taken so much time with her before.

As he languidly played in the folds of her sex, Penny began to unbutton her sweater. Robby, feeling the movement of her upper body, looked up to see what she was doing, slightly fearful that she was moving away from him. But it did not appear that way. Instead, she was slipping the sweater off her shoulders. Her breasts fell free. How beautiful they were! He had to touch them. But she was touching them. Her fingers sunk into the flesh of her breasts, kneading them, squeezing them. He stared at her, mesmerized. Her nipples rose a blood-brown color under the pinching pressure of her fingers. He reached up to touch them, hoping that she would not mind. No, of course she wouldn't mind, he thought briefly.

The flesh was soft, pliant. They were full and heavy in his hands. He lifted first one and then the other, as if weighing them. He encircled the nipple with his forefinger and thumb, squeezing it softly. Then, with the tip of his finger, he traced endless circles around it, just as he had moved his tongue around her clitoris. It was hard, rough feeling.

"My cunt, Robby," she moaned, "my cunt." Still holding onto one of her breasts, he took his head back to her cunt. He squeezed her breast hard, feeling the suppleness of it, while he darted his tongue inside her. He felt a strange kind of terror he hadn't known existed. It was the terror of the unknown. How would he know how to please her? How would he know if what he did felt good or bad to her? There was so much to learn. And as strange as the terror was, it was allayed by thrill, by the excitement of the unknown. He would just know, that's how, he thought. Of course he would know. If he knew what pleased him, then he would instinctively know what pleased her. He buried his face into her cunt again, drinking in the taste of her. Nothing was as good as this, nothing, and the terror served only to make it more pleasurable.

He kissed her clitoris, knowing somehow that this was the center of her sex, the source of her pleasure. Maybe he'd read it somewhere, maybe he knew by the way her buttocks moved on the couch when he touched it, maybe he knew by the way her thighs clamped around his head as he wrapped his lips firmly, but softly, around it. Yes, maybe that was it. She squirmed once again on the couch, her moans growing louder and more hoarse. He slid his lips, which were wet with both his saliva and her juices, back and forth over her clitoris. Her moans grew louder still.

Her hand fell over his on her breast and squeezed, urging him to squeeze her harder. He pinched her nipple between two fingers.

"Oh Robby, yes, yes!" she moaned when his tongue began to beat her clitoris back and forth by pushing into the base of it. "Yes, that's it, Robby, that's it." She could speak no more. The force of her quickly approaching orgasm was greater than any she'd ever known before. Her eyes flickered wildly beneath the thin shield of their lids. Blindness came, and then lightness—shards of yellow light piercing the blackness. Her body warmed and then weakened utterly. Robby, sensing finally that she was on the verge of orgasm by the way her buttocks moved, by the way her legs clamped his head firmly to her, began to gently suck on her clitoris.

"Oh, yes!" she screamed, unmindful of the open window. "Suck me like that, suck me." Looking up momentarily, he could see her face contorted in the passion of her pleasure—the pleasure she was receiving from him! He went back to her cunt, hungry for it, thirsty. Her hand came down and mingled with his tongue, her fingers moving into her cunt while he nibbled and sucked on her clitoris. She drew him tight with the power of her legs. He could not breathe, and yet he did not wish to breathe. He wanted only to give her pleasure. And then, he thought hazily, she will please me. His cock was hard and painfully digging into his trousers. He tried to rub it against the chair, but in his position he could not.

Her cunt was a bounty of delight, and soon he forgot his cock again and concentrated on her, though his ardor was most definitely linked with the throbbing of his cock. The orgasm was slow in coming, which made it all the more powerful, pleasurable and, indeed, agonizing. Each time Robby took his tongue away from her clitoris, the rising warmth that seemed ready to deluge through her body subsided until his tongue returned. It was painful. And yet the slow deliberation of it was more pleasurable than anything else. Her body was numb, her eyes twitching spastically, her limbs weightless.

She cupped her breasts in her hands and squeezed hard, and just then Robby took his tongue back to her clitoris and once again wrapped his lips around it. At the precise moment in which the bud of her sex was fully encircled by his lips, she exploded, calling out his name, pulsing endlessly to his tongue and bucking on the couch. Robby knew then that he was pleasing her.

She screamed. Her body leaped up as if it had been shocked. She thrust so forcefully that she almost knocked Robby backward. She reached for his head and pulled it between her thighs, his face against her pussy. The numbness in her fingers vanished. Her body began to shiver and tremble, and the seething sensations became more and more intense—so intense that she felt she would faint. She felt like laughing and crying at the same time.

And then, in a moment, it was all over.

Penny fell back against the couch. Robby, who had been on his knees, sat back and stared at her enthralled, his lips and chin glazed with saliva and her strangely sweet-tasting juices. She was moaning and talking to herself. She lay like a wet rag. Her beautiful breasts were heaving as if she'd run a race. Her nipples looked red and raw. From her pussy dribbled a milky-white substance similar to what exploded from him when he masturbated. Her hairs were all matted and soaking wet. She looked like a limp doll to him.

Her eyes opened slowly. He saw that her pupils were dilated. A soft smile came to her open lips. She licked them with her tongue. Then she raised one hand and brushed her long hair away from her face.

"Oh, darling. My darling Robby," she sighed, not

47

moving, her arms now at her sides, her legs still spread wide, her cunt still pulsing slightly. The black cushion on which she sat was slick with her wetness.

"Are you okay?"

"Yes. I'm all right. At least I think I am. I don't know what happened to me...but I'm okay, I guess."

"I hope so. You had me worried."

"I did?" She sat up a little with a bright smile on her face. "You were worried about me, Robby?"

"Yes."

"Oh, thank you. Thank you, Robby, for worrying."

He managed a little smile. She saw that he really was concerned.

"Come up here with me, Robby. I want you to hold me. I want to hold you in my arms. I want to kiss you for loving me. I want you close to me now, darling."

Robby's young heart buckled, almost splitting in half. He wanted to cry. This kind of tenderness was unknown to him. No one had ever spoken this gently to him. No one!

He sat down close to her. She folded him in her naked arms. Her breasts pressed into him, warming his flesh.

She kissed his perspiring brow. She kissed his closed eyes. He put his arms around her and held her tightly. She was still breathing rapidly, and he could feel her heart beating against his naked chest. He could feel the soft fullness of her damp breasts against his skin, and his hand came up to touch the sides of them, where they swelled out under the pressure of their contact.

She kissed his ears, and holding his face in her hands, she kissed his mouth. She could smell her own perfume on his burning face. She licked his lips and tasted her juices. She began to lick his entire face, even inserting the tip of her tongue up his nostrils. Then she forced his lips apart with her tongue and licked his teeth, again tasting her own come. She thrust her tongue deep into his mouth, and his tongue rose up to touch it. She drew his tongue into her mouth and sucked on it while her hands caressed his naked shoulders and his face.

She kept murmuring that she loved him, that he was precious to her. She thanked him again and again, and he began to laugh each time she said it. She kissed him gently, her hands running up and down his arms and across his expansive chest. She traced the outline of his ears tenderly, and then, moving the tips of her fingers from the lobe of his ear to his nose, she began to examine his face with them, as if she were blind. All the while, he lay peacefully in her naked arms, one elbow resting on her glorious breasts.

"Did you have a good time, Robby?" she asked, somewhat uncertain what his answer would be.

His eyes were closed and he was silent. Then he smiled. "Yes, Penny, I did. I don't know what came over me, but I did have a wonderful time."

"Do you feel guilty about it, Robby?"

"No. I guess not. Do you?"

"No. No." After a few moments of silence, she asked, "Do you want to sleep in bed with me tonight, Robby?"

He looked up into her eyes, and she kissed his nose. "I was going to ask you if I could, Penny. Can I?" he asked, his voice as innocent as his eyes.

"Yes, Robby. Yes. I want you to. I want you to stay with me tonight. I want to please you as you pleased me."

Chapter Six

Robby wanted to take a shower, and Penny put fresh towels out for him.

"Try not to be too long, Robby," she said, kissing his shoulders as she closed the door. She waited to see if he would lock it; he didn't.

In the living room she looked down at the couch, the scene of her first happiness in years. She felt warm all over, like a young girl. She was still slightly dizzy from the indescribably pleasurable and painful orgasm. And then she wondered: Was it normal for an orgasm to be painful? She wondered if something was wrong with her physical condition. But she quickly discarded these thoughts. Since the divorce, she'd been having all kinds of aches and pains, both real and imaginary. But successive medical checkups revealed nothing, the guarded prognosis always being the same, that her ills were psychosomatic.

Her whole body shuddered when she visualized herself slung back on the couch, her thighs spread, her hungry cunt exposed to a perfect stranger. She thought of Robby on his knees, his upper body naked and his darling face buried between her thrashing legs. She touched her pussy; it was sore, especially her clitoris. How terribly excited she'd been when he had first found it with his tongue and, realizing how sensitive it was, nibbled at it and finally, at her urging, sucked on it.

She was amazed he knew so much about the intricacies of a woman's anatomy. Where had he learned it? There was an art to it, and in a matter of minutes he had seemed to master it. He had known where and how to touch her, kissing her softly and then sucking hard, alternating to her inner thighs to let her cunt cool off and then returning at the right time, his magic mouth sending volcanic tremors through her body. It had seemed so natural to him. If she were his very first woman, that is, the first to expose her naked pussy to him, then Robby was phenomenal indeed! He knew exactly what to do, how to please and excite her. He was so eager and strong and agile.

She sighed deeply as she returned the couch to its original position. She put the Monopoly game back in the chest and then took the tray with the half-empty bottle and the glasses into her bedroom. She stripped off the quilt. She noticed that Clara had changed the bedding, and the sight of the freshly ironed sheets pleased her. She would do something nice for Clara.

"In here, Robby," she called out when she heard him leave the bathroom. Hearing his bare feet on the rug, she felt a renewed throbbing in her cunt. She cupped her heavy breasts and massaged them, stimulating her nipples. She dropped her hands when he appeared in the doorway, a towel around his waist. "Why don't you have a glass of wine and a cigarette while I bathe," she said, smiling.

He came closer to her nakedness, and they put their bare arms around each other, Robby hugging her close and kissing her chin. Her hands roamed over his damp back, her fingers touching the wet strands of his hair. The feel of his naked chest against her breasts caused her delicate pink nipples to harden, and she embraced him tightly. When she felt the slight pressure of his cock against her thigh, she almost gasped.

"Oh, Robby, you're a wretch! I must bathe, and then we have to get some sleep." She was teasing him, of course. She knew there would be little sleeping on either of their parts. The anticipation of being nude in bed with him was driving her insane with joy. Although she'd been up since eight that morning, she wasn't at all fatigued. Laughing, she escaped from his embrace and skipped down the corridor to the bath, conscious of his eyes caressing her naked buttocks as they flashed out of sight.

In the bathroom, she was impressed with Robby's neatness. He had carefully folded the towels he'd used, and the soap was in its cup and not left in the bottom of the tub as was Jeffrey's habit. His trousers were folded on top of his undershorts, and his socks were on top of those. She felt such warmth for the young man and appreciated his respect for her and his obvious pride in being well-mannered.

Penny was in and out of the shower swiftly. Removing the shower cap, she brushed out her long hair, admiring its length and body in the full-length mirror. She removed what little makeup she wore, creamed and cleansed her face, and then atomized her body from head to toe with the delicious fragrance of a special perfume, one she seldom used, but which always made her feel very sexy and desirable.

On the scale, she weighed 115 pounds. That was perfect. She stepped off, her body quivering slightly with anticipation, and slipped into a lemon-colored chiffon gown she rarely wore. It clung sheerly to her body, revealing in soft distillation the finest details and sweeping curves of her body. Turning to look at her backside in the mirror, she could see clearly the swell of her buttocks and the deep line bisecting them. She stepped into her toeless high-heeled slippers, from which her long legs stretched curvaceously. Then, whistling under her breath, she walked down the corridor into the bedroom.

"How do you feel, Robby?" she asked, standing close to the bed, lighting a cigarette.

"My jaw's beginning to ache." He smiled up at her, his eyes widening to the sight of her full, white breasts enshrouded in the filmy material of her gown. Her nipples, he could see, stood firm against it, threatening to poke through.

Penny laughed. "Oh, you poor thing. But it's no

wonder, is it? I don't know how you managed to keep licking for so long!"

"Neither do I. But I couldn't stop. I loved doing it." He lowered his eyes. "That was my first time. Did I do it okay? I've heard a lot about it, and I wanted to try it. Did I do it right, Penny?"

"Oh, my darling," she said, kneeling on the rug, kissing his face all over, letting him smell the perfume she wore. "You did beautifully. I must tell you too, Robby, you are the first man who's ever made me feel that good with his mouth and tongue," she said.

"You just called me a man," he grinned. "Did you mean that, Penny? You know, I'm not a man, not yet. At least, I don't feel like one."

"There's a lot of man in you, Robby. A lot of man. Few men are as gentle and as knowing as you." She got up and sat on the edge of the bed. He crawled over to her and arranged his head in her lap, looking up at her pretty face, one hand playing with her long hair.

"I'm happy to be here with you, Penny. I'm not lonely and I like how you trust me. Adults never trust young people, do they?"

"I trust you, darling," she said fondling his head and brushing his hair back from his dark eyes. She moved his head slightly and opened the lemon gown so that now her thighs were naked and the dark hair covering her warm pussy was visible. He smiled and rested his cheek on her milky-white flesh, his lips close to her fragrant bush. He bent forward and brushed his lips across her triangle of hair, and she felt a subtle spasm flicker in her body and then grow in intensity as his warm breath on her lower belly made her clitoris swell.

She extinguished her cigarette. She sipped from his wine glass and then placed it on the end table. She rested her hand on the sheet covering his thigh. He squirmed around and shifted onto his side as her hand caressed his body beneath the sheet. Finding his hairy armpit, she tickled him with her eager fingertips, and he giggled, his mouth now touching her throbbing mound.

She parted her legs slightly and felt her tender pussy lips spread open. The torment of passion again swept over her body, and she felt her cunt moisten as he started to kiss it more vigorously.

"You smell so delicious," he commented as she spread her legs open wider.

"Just lick gently this time, Robby. I'm a little irritated from your teeth, but it's okay. If you want, just lick softly. It makes me feel so wonderful. It almost makes me cry. Did you know that?"

He didn't answer. Carefully, he slipped his tongue between her outer pussy lips. He licked the insides of them, caressing her pink flesh with the tip of his tongue. Spreading them open, he rubbed his wetted lips up and down the length of them before sticking his tongue gently, softly, into her opening. He lingered there, tasting her, inhaling her delicious fragrance into his nostrils and swooning.

Her hand, beneath the sheet, spread over his chest to his belly. She could feel it tighten to her touch. He gasped and opened his legs slightly. How badly he wanted her to touch his cock, to wrap her fingers around it, to play with it. He was so tired of his own hand and couldn't even begin to fathom what a woman's touch would feel like. It throbbed against the sheet, aching to be held firmly.

She stretched the tips of her fingers down his belly, toward the uprising head of his cock. When they were fully extended, she brushed against the hot, smooth flesh at the head. Then she moved her arm down and began to rub her knuckles to the shaft, her fingers scratching his stomach and then trailing through his thick, coarse pubic hair. Robby began to moan slightly as he kept his tongue wiggling between her pouting pussy lips, his mouth half-open and his hot breath flowing inside her narrow opening.

Her desire was too great; she could tease him with her light touches no longer. She raised her hand away from his body and, spreading her fingers, lowered it again until she felt the heat of his flesh burning the palm of her hand. She squeezed, and he moaned as if she had squeezed the very air out of him. She measured it, her heart pumping, her fingers stretched along the length of the shaft. Then her palm closed around the head, gripping it firmly. Robby lurched and began to pump into her fist, rhythmically, forcefully, as she imagined he had pumped into his own fist many times before. Suddenly, white streams of semen spurted into her palm, his cock twitching and jerking in her grip.

"Oh Robby," she moaned, "Oh, yes!" She tossed back the sheet with her free hand. His cock was long and thick, and from it hot, white cream shot all over her hand and his belly. She covered the head with her other hand, and still the liquid came from a seemingly endless wellspring deep within him. His cock was strong and hard in her hand, the veins pumping as she gripped him firmly. She massaged the head of it, rubbing her palm around and around it until his spasms calmed somewhat.

"Just lie still, dear," she said, looking up at his tormented face. His eyes were clamped shut, his body shivering, his prick still pumping and throbbing in her gentle hands.

Robby couldn't fathom what had happened, why it had happened so quickly. This wasn't his first orgasm, but the few others he'd worked himself into by masturbating against a satin-covered pillow, rubbing his penis until it erupted, had been unsatisfying and the sensations he'd experienced afterward were frustrating.

It seemed to him that there had been no warning that he was going to shoot. It just happened. The feel of her warm hand and her tickling fingers; the closeness of her moist, sweet-smelling pussy to his lips and tongue; the idea that they were both naked; the memory of having sucked her on the couch, having looked up her skirt, having seen and touched her lovely breasts; and the sensation of her lusting against his anxious mouth had all crashed into one terrific image, and that was when he'd lost control and come all over her gripping fingers.

Now he felt a relentless guilt overwhelming him. He wished he could vanish. He was blushing, he knew, and he was ashamed. He had never been more embarrassed!

Penny quickly fell into his arms and held him close. She kissed his lips and his cheeks. She almost sensed what he was feeling.

"It's all right...it's all right, baby...it's all right. What happened was natural. Don't screw your face up that way. I tell you, it's normal, Robby. It was beautiful!"

"I think I should go home, Penny," he murmured. "I think I should. I feel so bad."

"Oh, darling! Robby, listen, listen to me. It's natural. Your penis just did what it should do. Didn't I have an orgasm because of your marvelous tongue? Didn't you suck me into coming? You did, you know, and that was beautiful too. It was very, very beautiful, Robby. Darling, believe me. Come now, relax your body and let me kiss you and let me touch your cock again." She smiled. "Maybe we can make it hard again, even harder than it was, and then you can come again and maybe even again. You'll see, Robby, how sweet it is and how I love it, and how you'll love it, too."

"Let me go to the bathroom and wash, please," he said, starting to get up.

"Oh no, Robby," she said. "Just lie back and relax, and I'll clean you, okay, darling? I'll clean you."

A great shudder passed through his body and he

57

shook violently for a moment. Penny pushed the sheet all the way down to his naked feet, and then she bent over him, brushing her hair back as she did. Lying naked, his cock stirred on his belly, rising into the cool air. How good it felt to be thus exposed. With a coy grin on her face, she leaned over him and began to lick his thighs which were spotted with his sperm. It was salty and warm. She moved up to his balls and began to lick them too. Robby groaned deeply. Never had he imagined a feeling quite as exquisite as that; her tongue was wet and warm and soft as it tickled him, soothed him, caressed him. His cock shot up into the air. She kissed the base of his cock, burying her lips in his thick bush. Moving her lips upwards along the length of his shaft, she noticed how it jerked this way and that way, wanting, she knew, to be held firmly by her mouth. At the top, she slipped her cool lips around the strong, velvet head.

She used her tongue to wash his burning crown, licking all around the rim and flicking across the slit in its tip. When he began to gasp from the intense sensations, she allowed the shaft to slip down her throat, working her muscles so that they massaged his turgid flesh.

Robby's eyes rolled back in his head and he groaned. Penny could feel him stiffen still more, and she relaxed her hold on his cock. She let it slip back into her mouth and slashed along the underside of the shaft with the end of her tongue, finally working her way down to his balls. She took them in her mouth one at a time and worried them, pulling on them gently and rolling them between her lips. He swelled more and more as she took him fully into her mouth again, bobbing her head up and down, swallowing him.

"Oh, oh, Penny," he gasped, holding the sides of her head with his hands. "It's happening again! It's...going to explode...I'm going to come."

Penny simply smiled and continued to pump him with her lips and throat. She used long strokes, pulling back so that practically all of him emerged from her mouth before she swallowed him again.

Then Robby came. In four great spurts his hot sperm shot down her throat. The quantity wasn't so great as when she'd used her hand on him, but he still managed to make her take two or three swallows before she could get it all down. She continued to tug on his cock until the last thick drops spilled onto her tongue.

Penny let his diminishing cock fall from between her lips. She smiled and stretched and took his face in her hands, kissing him and letting him taste the saltiness of his own sperm. "You, my dear," she said, "aren't bad at all for a beginner."

Chapter Seven

After morning had dawned and the grandfather clock was sounding nine golden chimes, Robby slowly opened his sleepy eyes. He could smell the appetizing aroma of bacon. The odor of freshly brewed coffee filled the bedroom. He was alone, stretched out naked, the sheet down at the foot of the bed. He had a fantastic hard-on, as he did every morning upon waking. He rolled on his side, brushing his erect penis against the bed. He grabbed the pillow next to his and buried his face in it, smelling Penny's wonderful perfume. Almost automatically, he placed the pillow between his legs and began to rub his long cock against the coolness of the pillowcase. Then he remembered the previous night and quickly replaced the pillow. He saw some of her long hairs on it and kissed them reverently. He started to think about how he'd fallen asleep while she was mouthing his prick, but these thoughts were almost too precious, too secret to resurrect. He wanted to keep them, like a valuable treasure, all to himself, savoring each and every one of them, gently uncovering them as the days passed, worshipping them like little gods. He often did this with scenes from very special books he read. It was like making a date with himself to think about this or that thing, especially when he was alone, smoking in the park.

Oh, how lucky, how fantastically lucky he'd been, meeting Penny in the park! It was like something out of a fairy tale. He still couldn't believe some of what had happened.

He sat up and touched his penis. He ran his fingers over the satiny head. He talked to it quietly. "You know, pecker,"—which was what he called it privately—"you've been inside a woman's mouth. Do you realize that, pecker? Inside, her tongue all over you, her lips kissing all of you from the top down to your balls...your very own balls she kissed and licked, pecker." His penis throbbed in seeming acknowledgment of this truth.

He flicked his index finger and thumb at the swollen head. "Come on now, behave yourself, because I've got to piss. I can't piss with you hard like this, pecker." He flicked it again and again until it seemed to understand and began to shrink back to normal size.

But then, despite everything, the image of Penny's legs spread open to his mouth came back to him, and his cock rose to meet his belly. This time he didn't bother speaking to it. Instead, imagining her pink, moist flesh, he wrapped his fingers around it. He rubbed it up and down, the loose skin moving in increments with his palm as if stuck to it. He thought of her mouth slipping down over his cock as his hand bore down and pressed to the base of it. He thought of her tongue spiraling around the head, and with his forefinger and thumb he encircled it just below the thick ridge at the top. He lay back and inhaled her sweet fragrance. He thought of her body and came, exploding into his cupped palm, his thighs hard with tension, his stomach taut. His body jerked on the bed, and when his shudders stopped, he spread the cream into his belly, hoping that later she would lick him clean.

As he went into the bathroom and closed the door, he heard the tinkling sound of dishes and silverware. He first became conscious of this breakfast-time music when he raised the toilet seat and guided his cock toward the bowl. Sunlight was streaming through the stained-glass window near the tub, lighting up the design in the shower curtain and falling into a large hexagonal pattern on the thick, green rug which partially covered the tiled floor. The whole bathroom smelled like Penny. He saw the lemon-colored gown she'd worn hanging on the back of the door. Her high-heeled slippers were near the scale.

Never in his life, as physically comfortable and relatively uncomplicated as it was, had he felt more at home than he did now. It almost seemed as if he belonged here! He turned and saw his trousers suspended from the pants hanger on a hook in the tiled wall. The shoes he had kicked off were on the floor. Penny had rinsed out his wash-and-wear undershorts. They were folded on top of his shoes.

He smiled at his reflection in the mirror. He was proud of his healthy, athletic body. He studied his penis and testicles and fondled them, grinning. God, he thought to himself, what a priceless time I've had! His cock started to stiffen again, and he spoke to it. "Here now, pecker, as you were, at ease! Maybe you can have more fun later. I don't know. I also don't know what the girl's thinking about. And you know how girls are, pecker, don't you? Remember that one in back of the bus coming from the hockey game up at school? Remember her? She let me have a kiss and you jumped up and then she ran and sat with the other guy. And you got mad and started getting harder and harder, and finally, while I watched this jerk kissing her and casually playing with her breasts, you spit all over. Remember that, pecker? So behave yourself!"

He weighed himself. As he stood on the scale, he saw a sheet of paper taped to the wall. On it was written the date and then her weight. He took the pencil and printed his initials and his weight next to hers. He was just twenty neat pounds heavier than her 115. He dressed, and went out into the living room. It was hard to believe that this was the scene of the wonderful crime! He wouldn't mind living here at all, was his thought when he heard Penny's voice behind him.

"Good morning!"

He turned from examining the books. "Hello.

Good morning." Penny was fully dressed. She wore a soft, yellow sweater; her nipples were hard against the material. A pair of very short shorts clung to her buttocks and outlined her pussy mound so that he could see every curve of it. Her pretty feet were bare.

"You sleep like a little baby, Robby. A kidnapper could take you away and you'd never know it."

"My father says I sleep like a water-soaked log."

"I like sleeping babies better, especially when they're as handsome as you are," she grinned, remembering how she'd sucked his cock as his eyes had closed, how she'd spent a long time licking it and swirling it around inside her mouth, hoping it would harden. But it hadn't because Robby had fallen into a deep sleep, the strong sherry having knocked him out.

While he slept, she had licked all of his precious, good-tasting sperm from her hand and fingers and then from his thighs. She had sucked on his balls, taking them into her mouth, loving the sensation of his two testes as she tongued and swallowed them and then let them escape from her hot mouth, watching them shrink and then expand and then move and squirm as the tip of her tongue teased them.

She had never been so intimate with any man!

Thinking about it stirred up new passions in her body, and she deliberately chased the thoughts away. "If it's okay with you, buster, I'm acting the part of your wife this morning." She put her hands on his shoulders, her smiling face close to his. "I cooked your breakfast is what I mean."

He laughed. "I'd rather you be my wife than my mother. She always scared me and she never fixed breakfast. Never."

"I don't feel like your mother, Robby."

"Well, you certainly don't remind me of her," he said as her lips brushed across his cheek.

"Did you find the extra toothbrush I put out for you?"

He said he hadn't seen it, and she told him where it was. He brushed his teeth as she watched him happily. Then they ate breakfast together in the kitchen. Penny was quite impressed with his table manners. This is a well-bred kid, she said to herself, again thanking her stars for the remarkable good luck they had showered upon her.

"I guess you have to go home now," she said, accepting a light for her cigarette.

"It might not be a bad idea. I've never stayed out all night. One of the neighbors might notice and report me to my father. But I doubt that. Our house is a very quiet one."

"You can stay with me for awhile if you wish; I don't have anything important to do today." Penny had nothing important to do any day. And she hated it. While cooking she had tried to think up some way to entertain him, to keep him with her. She had wanted to think of something that wasn't sexual, though an erotic encounter would have been just as satisfactory, if not more so. In fact, she thought, she would be more than happy to strip naked right now and drag him into her bed and spend all day and all night with his magnificent body and his strong, hard, throbbing prick. But she had made up her mind not to seduce him any further, having even debated whether she should wear a brassiere to conceal her tingling nipples, at which he stared from time to time while they were eating.

"Yeah, I guess we could talk awhile. I've got a hundred questions I'd like to ask, Penny." He blushed. "They're all about sex. You know, that's all I think about sometimes. I spend a lot of time..."

"We all do, Robby. All of us."

"Like now. I can't stop thinking about it. What made me feel so good...sucking you...I mean, you know, feeling you so hot and so soaking wet in your...in your..."

"Pussy, Robby. Say 'pussy.'"

"In your pussy, in your pussy." He glanced up. "I can't say 'cunt'?"

"If you like, say 'cunt.' I like 'pussy' better. I don't know why, but I do. 'Cunt' is kind of a hard word, but I don't dislike it. It's vulgar-sounding, but I must admit that sometimes I secretly like vulgar things and vulgar words."

"Like 'fuck'?"

"Yes, darling. Yes. I like that word very much. It means something wonderful. And it's so dirty it makes me shiver...kind of feel wet and slippery inside my little pussy. Like now it's making me wet inside my pussy just from talking about it."

"And it makes me hard," he acknowledged quite matter-of-factly.

"Are you hard now?"

"Yes, 'pecker's' hard."

"Do you call your penis 'pecker'?"

"That's his name," Robby grinned. "I've always called him that." He looked at her strangely. "Do you have a name for your pussy?"

She smiled. "No. I've never given it a name. To tell the truth, my pussy's been almost a stranger to me, that is, until last night when you taught me something I didn't think I'd ever learn. You know what you taught me? You taught me to like it, not to be afraid of it, to let it loose, free, let it go and feel what it wants to feel, instead of holding back the way I've always done."

"While you were married, too?"

"Yes. Since I was little and I had my first period. You see, it always hurt, and when I had intercourse with my husband it always hurt, and even when I'd touch it, you know..." she lowered her eyes, a faint blush covering her face, "you know...when you play with yourself sometimes...well, it would hurt even then."

"Oh," he said and lapsed into silence.

"Is your cock very hard?"

"Very." She watched as his hand crept between his legs and his fingers touched it. "It's getting even harder," he muttered innocently, a look of surprise in his eyes. "I guess it's all this sex talk doing it."

"Could I see it?" Her eyes were soft and smoldering.

"Oh, sure. Sure you can see it, Penny." He started to stand up and open his fly, but she told him to stay seated.

Grinning like a happy child, she sat down on the floor directly in front of him. "Can I take it out, Robby? I'd like to do that. Let me?"

Looking down at her loveliness sitting so close him, the shining white flesh of her bare legs and the provocatively concealed mound of her pussy, a fierce shivering overwhelmed him and he felt goose pimples breaking out all over.

He spread his legs around her body, gripping her between them, his eyes glued to her voluptuous breasts and her nipples straining against the soft cashmere. She slowly unzipped his fly. His cock was fully erect, standing up against his belly inside his underwear. Grinning and licking her lips languorously, she reached inside his shorts and took hold of his rod, her fingers wrapping around it. Feeling the heat of it, her body melted against his strong legs. She used her free hand to pull down his shorts. The huge prick, his beloved pecker, leaped into the air. She grabbed for it again and clutched it in her fist.

"Oh, Robby," she sighed, "it's so hard. It's so beautiful. It's a marvelous prick, just marvelous." She sighed again and bent her head to kiss his thighs. She licked the inner flesh of them, moving slowly up, teasing him, his cock expanding as her lips moved nearer to his balls. Then, with his eyes closed, he shuddered to feel the tip of her tongue come out to trace a feathery touch from the underside of his balls to the base of his cock. And then he felt nothing. Opening his eyes, he gasped, for her lips were falling onto the head of his cock, slipping over it, and the whole of him was held, in a blissful instant, fully and warmly inside her wet mouth. She sucked hard, seeming to take his entire body down her throat, holding him, urging him to the extreme limit of pleasure. And in another instant, which was as quick and surprising as the one preceding it, she withdrew her mouth from him.

She kissed his cock then, kissing around the ridge of the head, up and down the length of him, her lips pressing into the blue vein which ran along the underside. He opened his eyes when he felt her lips pull away from him again.

"I want you to touch my breasts with it," she said, pulling her sweater up to her neck to expose her luscious white breasts to his eyes. Shifting closer to him, she placed his throbbing penis into the valley between her breasts. She pressed them together, holding his cock firmly but softly there, hiding it, secreting it away. She could feel the velvety head, hot against her warm flesh. Robby began to push into the deep crevice, to urge his hardness into her softness. As he pushed deeper in, pulled out and pushed in again, she continued to squeeze her breasts together, to make for him the softest bed possible.

It was Robby who withdrew this time, pulling his cock out from the warm cleavage and circling the head of it around her hardened nipples as if he were painting her areolas a deeper color of rose. Her eyes rolled back in her head momentarily, and slowly she came to focus on him again, on the red bulb of his sex drawing endless circles around her aching nipples.

She licked her palm, wetting it with her saliva, and

closed it around his cock. She ran her hand up and down it smoothly, making it glisten. Then she guided it back between her breasts, saying, "Fuck my breasts, Robby." He breathed deeply and began to thrust upwards into the deep space provided by her hands pressing her delectable melons together. He watched her face as he pumped in and out of the crevice; it was placid and yet tense at once. How did it feel, he wondered, to have one's breasts fucked? But he could not think, for his own pleasure was too great.

Her flesh was soft, full and warm. It seemed to encompass not only his cock, but his entire being as well. He felt held by her, enclosed within her. His buttocks expanded and contracted on the cold seat of the chair as he pushed deeper in and withdrew from the space between her breasts. She wet his cock again, and he thrust forward. As he was about to come he pinched her nipples hard, causing her to moan. Feeling the hard, pebble-like nipples between his thumb and forefinger, he buried himself deep within her, her breasts shaking with his increasingly violent motions, her mouth gaping open, her eyes closed. In the intensity of his pleasure he could not hold his eyes open to see his come wetting her white flesh, her chin, her lips. He could feel only the deep, soft, giving flesh of her breasts enclosed around him, absorbing the agonizing throbbing of his cock.

Chapter Eight

Afterwards, Penny massaged Robby's fluids into her skin, looking at him all the while. Then, as she moved to put her sweater back on, Robby stopped her.

"Please," he said, "keep it off. I want to look at you while I eat." And so she kept her sweater off and sat back down at the table. As he ate, his eyes stayed fixed on her breasts; they glowed translucently from the wetness of his release which she'd rubbed all over them. On her nipple there was still a creamy drop of his come. To that he looked as he drank his juice. Later, he thought, he would lick it off. It would be his dessert. He'd never had dessert with breakfast before.

Penny was in agony. She had loved the feel of his cock pumping in and out of her breasts. She wanted more. She wanted to feel the same sensations in her cunt. She wanted him to fuck her with the same ardor he had given to her breasts. She squirmed in her chair, trying to shift her skirt so that her cunt would lie directly upon it, soothed perhaps by the coolness of the wooden seat. She waited for him to finish eating. It seemed the moment would never arrive.

Finally, he wiped the napkin across his full lips and threw it to the table. "Now what should we do?" he asked lightly. "Still want to talk?" She laughed and walked over to him. She kneeled before him again as his cock began stirring on his thighs. She took it, still soft, directly between her lips and felt it expand to the dimensions of her mouth. In an instant he was hard again, the tip of his cock touching the back of her throat. He moaned. Slowly, she slid her mouth up the length of it until the swollen head rested gently on her lips. She licked the tip with gentle strokes, clutching the base tightly. With her other hand she lightly tickled his balls. Instinctively, he thrust forward in an effort to have his cock more firmly held by her.

She held it lightly in her mouth, tickling him, spiraling her tongue around and around the base. His heart beat loudly, and he was certain that she could hear it, that it thundered through the room. Releasing him, she began to lick up and down the length of his shaft, her rapid motions like wildfire, her fingers like the wind. She kissed the side of it, pressing it to his belly as she did, so that that pressure alone was almost enough to make Robby come again.

And then she took her warm, wet mouth away and looked up to him, admiring his wonderful boyish features: his sensual mouth, his blood-red lips, his sculpted nose. She squeezed his cock, pumping her hand up and down it to see how his face would respond. She was pleased with the response, for his eyes fluttered, his mouth twitched in both agony and pleasure. Her own cunt burned.

"Robby, I want to fuck you. I want your cock inside me, fucking me, filling me. Would you like that, Robby?" Her voice was unearthly, hoarse.

"Oh God," he moaned, "Oh God, yes." His body trembled as she put renewed vigor into her sucking. "Yes, I want to fuck you, I'll fuck you." But he was frightened; he didn't know how, he had never fucked a woman before. What if he did it wrong, what if he were awkward and child-like? But her mouth, slipping wetly down the length of him, made him forget his fears, forget even what she had asked. "Oh, God, don't ever stop," he moaned, his cock throbbing on her tongue. His words came out in a choking, throaty whisper. "Don't ever stop."

She stopped and looked up at him, smiling. "You want to fuck me, don't you?" Her words were almost painful to him. "It feels as good, even better, than this," she said as she slipped her full lips down the length of him again. "Just wait, you'll see. When you slip your cock into me, you'll forget that you don't know how. It's as natural as anything in the world. You'll feel things you never dreamed of feeling. I'll lie beneath you," she continued, fondling his hard cock and looking directly into his eyes, "and I'll spread my legs as wide as you like. Then you can enter me slowly, as slow as you need, as slow as it gives you pleasure to enter me, and I'll close around you, my cunt—there's your word—will close around you, wrap around your hardness. You can go in as deep as you like, and as hard as you like, because my pussy will be wet. I'll teach you as you go along, and I'll probably learn some new things myself.

"Don't be afraid, Robby. Remember last night when you licked me on the couch, when you sank your tongue deeply into me? Remember how I responded? Remember how wet I got, how I pressed my cunt to your face because it felt so good, remember?" Robby nodded, and she continued, caressing the smooth skin of his cock with her fingertips. "Remember how hungry I was for you? Well, now I'm hungrier. Now I want you to fuck me, fuck me, Robby. Now I want you to fuck me with this wonderful cock, darling. I want you to climb on top of me and thrust into me, to bury yourself deeply within me." Speaking like this was enough to make Penny come. She was certain that if she touched her fingers to her cunt, rubbed her clitoris for even a second, she would do just that. She gripped his cock and squeezed it as if to punctuate her little speech.

"Yes, Penny," he moaned, closing his eyes to the pressure of her hand, "yes, I want to fuck you with my cock." And then he began to writhe on the kitchen chair as her mouth closed once again over his flaming prick. "Yes, oh yes, Penny, fuck me, fuck me like that." Slowly, she stood up, her eyes never leaving his thick, throbbing prick. She slid down her white shorts, wriggling her buttocks as she did. Then they were around her ankles, and the black triangle of her cunt hair was inches away from him—her lovely cunt. He loved it, he loved her. Her cunt was his.

He let her pull him up by the hands. He took off his socks and shoes, tossing them carelessly to the side. He was shaking. His cock stood jerking against his muscular, tight stomach, the tip of it leaking slightly. His buttocks were clenched as tight as his balls. Penny kneeled before him and began to rub her long, silky hair up and down his cock. He unbuttoned his shirt as he looked down at his cock, which was now entangled in her hair, only the red tip of it showing through.

"Let's fuck right here, Robby," she said, pulling him down to the floor with her. "Fuck me here on the kitchen floor. I couldn't endure the long walk to the bedroom; I can't wait that long to have your cock inside me." She lay supine on the cold floor, her arms reaching out to him, pulling him down on top of her. Her legs spread, and his knees pushing them even further apart. His mouth was open in total amazement at his good fortune, his eyes half-lidded. He moved onto her perspiring body, his chest pressing into her ripe breasts. He could feel her hard nipples burning into his own.

His cock slipped between her thighs and she squeezed them together, rubbing him with her tender, hot flesh. He could have come then. She opened her legs then and, taking his cock into her hand, guided it to the entrance of her cunt. She rubbed the head of it back and forth over the surface of her sex, wetting the smooth flesh completely, exquisitely. Robby wanted to thrust into her, but waited, letting the more experienced Penny lead the way. But still, he felt as if his prick were going to explode in her hands.

The entrance to her cunt was slippery, warm, and

he could hardly contain the sensations of having his cock rubbed along it like that. Gently, he pushed into her, the round bulb of his cock slipping just between the folds of her cunt. She held him there, still swirling him around her circular entrance.

"Yes, Robby, that's how, that's how my darling, push it in, push it in." Robby pushed further in. "Don't hurry darling. Don't hurry. I can feel the head now between my lips. I can feel it slipping in. Oh, it feels so good, Robby." Robby lingered there, feeling the slow ecstasy of envelopment. He pushed still further in, burying the head entirely within her walls. His cock throbbed, expanding as it moved into her. She moaned and reached her arms behind him, his firm, athletic buttocks, pressing him to her, her fingers sinking into his flesh.

Penny's breath came faster as his prick slowly filled her. Each time Robby gave a gentle push—still barely able to contain himself, yet determined to let Penny guide him—she bore down slightly on his cock, spreading her thighs wider. And then, as if he had suddenly realized what he was doing, that he was lying on top of a woman, fucking her, he thrust deeply into her, his cock buried up to the balls. Penny let out a deep-throated moan and heaved her hips upwards, lifting her buttocks off the ground.

"Oh, yes, Robby, that's perfect, that's just perfect." Her breath was hot in his ear and seemed to cause him to begin pumping in and out of her. He pulled his cock out and thrust back in, and each time he did, Penny said, "Yes, yes." Her legs came up and wrapped around his waist, bringing her mound harder against the base of his cock as it massaged her fiery clitoris. She began, with her buttocks rising and falling from the floor, to pump in unison with him.

Her fingernails dug into his flesh, causing him to think momentarily about the pain, and then his body warmed and the pain was forgotten, though still, her

nails sank deeply into the flesh of his buttocks. She
scratched them up and down his back, causing him to
writhe on top of her. He drove into her, bearing down
hard once fully inside, and withdrew. He pumped
hard and fast, oblivious to everything, including his
fear. His balls slapped her thighs and the crevice
beneath her cunt. Penny arched her back, lifting his
entire body along with hers, and then fell hard back
to the cold floor, his body coming heavy down on
hers, his cock moving deeply into her.

"Kiss me Robby, kiss me. I want your tongue in
my mouth, I want to taste you, to suck your tongue."
Robby's head came down like a shadow over her
face, and he kissed her, thrusting his tongue into her
mouth, while at the same time pulling his cock to the
opening of her cunt and driving back in. His hand
came up and grasped her breast. He squeezed it.

"Harder, Robby, harder!" He didn't know if she
meant her breast or his fucking, so he did both, slamming into her and squeezing her breast as hard as he
could.

"Oh darling, I'm going to come all over your hot
prick, all over it." Her words faded into something
more akin to a groan as she thrust her hips against
his and rotated them, his cock held fully by her cunt.
"Oh fuck me, fuck me like that!" she yelled, her cunt
beginning to pulse against his now throbbing cock.

She bounced on the floor, her orgasm sweeping
over her in endless waves, her cunt absorbing him,
sucking him in. Feeling the strange motions of her
body beneath him, Robby could no longer contain
himself, and exploded against the far wall of her sex.
They clutched each other, pressing their bodies tightly together, and moved into oblivion.

Afterwards, Robby opened his eyes as if waking
from a dream. She raised her head and kissed him
deeply, her tongue stretching to the back of his
throat. "That was wonderful, darling," she purred,

her lips coming away from him. He smiled with the infinite knowledge of her body—the infinite, new knowledge of sex. He wondered if he had been alive before then, or if he had been, rather, sleep-walking through his days.

"I want to lick your cunt now," he said, fondling her breasts. "Would you like that?"

"Oh, my darling," she exclaimed, hugging him. "Oh, Robby, let's wait, let's please wait. Yes, you can suck my pussy...my cunt in a little while...but I must rest for a moment. You don't understand what all this does to me. It's the most thrilling, the most wonderful sensation on earth, isn't it?"

"Yes," he said somewhat impatiently, "but I just want to kiss it, to taste us," he said plaintively, slowly withdrawing his still-hard prick.

Penny almost collapsed as she felt the long, thick, hot shaft leave the dark wetness of her still-vibrating cunt. "Oh, Robby, my sweet. Yes. Yes, my darling. You can taste us, yes, kiss me."

Wordlessly, Robby slid between her damp thighs. His penis still towering and primed for more action, he lay on his stomach and buried his face in her drenched pussy, kissing furiously as Penny threw her legs wide open.

His tongue slid effortlessly along the outer folds of her cunt, which were soaked with the wetness of their release. He sucked at her opening, drinking from her. Lightly, he ran his tongue over her raw clitoris. She lurched back from it. He came forward and breathed onto it, soothing it with warm air. And then he touched it again, very gently with just the tip of his tongue, and despite the pain, Penny felt herself pushing against him, her body warming, flooding with yet another orgasm. In seconds, she was moaning and coming onto his tongue, his lips. He drank thirstily, lapping at her cunt and drinking in every last drop of her come.

Chapter Nine

Robby stayed most of that morning. Neither of them put their clothing back on, and like children playing happily on the beach, they reveled in the freedom of their nakedness.

All morning he chased her around playfully, sometimes quite purposefully, wanting to fuck her time and time again. She kept pleading with him to give her time to rest. At first it was a laughing matter, his teasing her, holding his enlarged cock in his hand and rubbing it against her pussy hair whenever he could get the chance. This was the child-with-the-new-toy syndrome, Penny explained to herself when she began to lose patience with him, but she couldn't successfully explain it to Robby.

"Oh, come on, Penny, let me stick it in for just a minute or so. Look, I promise to take it out. I won't hurt you. I promise."

He tried valiantly to capture her pussy from the rear while she was bending to pick up some clothes from the floor. When she moved away from him, he rubbed his cock instead between the cheeks of her ass. For a moment she relented and let him slide it up and down the dark crevice. Within seconds she could feel his hot liquid shooting onto her buttocks.

When she asked him afterwards what time he'd planned on leaving, he told her he didn't have to leave until about noon, when he expected a visit from a school chum who was to return some books he'd borrowed for the summer. Inspired, she tried to encourage him to read something, but Robby couldn't be distracted. After having come onto her buttocks, he wanted to fuck her cunt from behind.

Instead, she offered to suck him until he had his orgasm, but he didn't want that. "No," he explained,

"I want to fuck your hot cunt," and she cringed in anticipation of the pain.

Finally, she relented altogether. She was getting annoyed at his begging, his pleading. On the verge of yelling at him, she told him he could fuck her again, but that he couldn't do it from behind, explaining that she was too sore and that that would only exacerbate her pain.

She lay down on the bed, already naked, and spread her legs. This she was doing for him. She really wasn't in the mood; the burning pain in her cunt from all those years of disuse was too great. And Robby's virgin fuck had been violent, ripping through her like a storm. But she was sick of his pleading. And anyway, wasn't it her cunt that had started this whole thing?

He climbed eagerly on top of her and parted the lips of her cunt with his fingers. His touch was gentle, respectful of her pain, and for that she was glad. Slowly, he entered her, careful not to rub too hard against her raw flesh. As soon as he was completely inside her, he began to sway back and forth, to move himself in nearly indiscernible circles within her walls. She felt nothing but pleasure and remarked how much he'd learned in so short a time.

In this position, his cock bearing down on her clitoris, her cunt filled by him, she began to feel the beginnings of another orgasm. She closed her eyes and began to move her hips back and forth, to raise her legs into the air, to allow him more freedom to move within her.

The orgasm was slow and languorous, and as it rose, so too, did it rise in Robby. He stayed buried within her, still moving slowly, still afraid of hurting her. He didn't know of her pleasure, but sensed it when she gripped his waist tightly with her thighs and moaned softly. Then he came, his cock unmoving inside her, his lips pressed to her neck, thanking her.

Dressing, she explained to him that what she really needed to do was to take a long, hot bath. She told him again that it had been a long time since she'd been fucked like that, both complimenting him and getting her message across at once, and that yes, she had enjoyed the last fuck very much. At last he understood, his need abated somewhat by their last slow session. Still, he was anxious to know when she'd be ready to fuck again. He couldn't help it, he said, assuming a look of little boy helplessness, "I just want to fuck your beautiful cunt."

She told him she guessed that by evening she'd be feeling more like it, but that now she desperately needed a rest. He acquiesced calmly, his well-mannered self overruling his wild desires for her voluptuous body and her hot, juicy cunt.

She fed him lunch early, and he ate wolfishly. She enjoyed sitting at the table watching him. She'd made herself a scotch and they chatted about numerous things, mostly sex. His persistent questions centered on the origins of orgasm; why nipples hardened; what the clitoris was made of; why the female's asshole was so close to her pussy; whether adult men ever got them mixed up, putting their cock up the wrong hole; and if they did, whether it felt good or if it hurt much. He wanted especially to know whether girls liked it that way because he had heard up at school that they did.

Penny answered all of his questions as honestly as she could. She didn't know the answers to many of them. When she began to tell him about anal-eroticism, knowing, indeed, something about it, she felt a tingling sensation in her cunt. Her asshole, strangely, began to itch, and as she talked about it, telling him that there were certain people who found the anus very erotic, women included, the itching became unbearable so that she began to squirm imperceptibly in her seat.

Robby's young, curious mind, however, raced ahead of her, leaving her behind with her memories of a distant experience. As he talked on about masturbation and things he'd heard from some boys at school about homosexuality, she let her mind wander to the first time that she'd discovered just how erotic that part of her body was to her.

It had been in college when she'd had her first experience with a woman, her roommate Kathryn. Nothing had really happened, she recalled, hearing Robby's voice drone on in the background, but there had been that night when she'd been sleeping and Kathryn had slipped into bed with her. Shocked, she'd felt the young woman's hands coming up the side of her body to touch her breasts, caressing the line of her neck, the fingertips running over her slightly parted lips. And then suddenly, she'd felt the finger of Kathryn's other hand on her naked buttocks.

Just thinking about it caused Penny's loins to stir. Nothing had happened, except that Kathryn had then touched her asshole. How strange, she'd thought at the time, that she should crawl into bed with me just to touch my asshole. Of course, her other hand, draped over Penny's side, had lingered on her breast, but really all it had seemed that Kathryn wanted to do was to touch her asshole. She'd traced the circle of it over and over with her finger, dipping it into the dark space only slightly. And she'd left it there, her finger buried a little way in, and had fallen asleep. Penny, though, had remained awake for a good hour, wondering about the strange sensations flooding her body, about why Kathryn had felt compelled to do that. She'd squeezed her muscles around the girl's fingers, feeling the odd pressure, becoming aroused. And then finally, she too had fallen asleep. Penny smiled at the memory, but Robby didn't notice, so wound up was he in his own story.

When the grandfather clock chimed twelve, Robby stood and said he had to leave. It was at this very moment, when the announcement fell from his sensual lips, that she felt a kind of panic. She suddenly felt very lonely.

"When will I be seeing you again, Robby?"

"Oh, I guess later. You know, Penny, when you feel better. Maybe tonight. Maybe tomorrow. Oh, I don't know."

This was the way young men always behaved, she remembered; the tone of his casual answer was reminiscent of the unthinking cruelty exhibited by children. He wasn't at all angry with her. He was taking her necessary rejection of his sexual offers quite calmly. In fact, he seemed to have lost all interest in her. Although she wore the yellow sweater and her perfect breasts were outlined so beautifully, hinting at their nakedness beneath the soft hugging fabric, he scarcely stared at them any more. Earlier, he hadn't been able to pull his eyes away from her stiff nipples, which showed clearly through the fine material.

She was sitting on the chair next to him, sipping from her scotch, one naked leg bent and her bare toes balanced on the edge of the seat. Looking down, she could see curly tendrils of her dark pussy hairs creeping out from the edges of her tight shorts. He'd been absolutely fascinated with these hairs earlier, pulling on them playfully, loving her reactions of pretended pain. But his eyes had not glanced at her crotch once during the long sex conversation.

In a way, Penny found him traditionally adultlike in his treatment of her, which was almost standoffish at times. It made her regret not fucking him more.

"Well, will you call me?" she asked, hating the sound of weakness in her voice.

"Oh, sure. Sure, sure! I'll call you. What's your number?"

She hated him suddenly for the casual tone of his

voice. But she laughed and understood. Boys were boys and there was no changing that. She berated herself for having envisioned some kind of semi-permanent, if not altogether permanent, relationship with him. Wasn't she being quite foolish?

He dressed and left, almost forgetting to say good-bye. She had to remind him twice to take the telephone number she'd written on a slip of paper.

"Robby?" He was going out the door. He stopped and turned to her, grinning.

"Yes, Penny?" He gave her the distinct impression that she was delaying him.

"Robby, are you going out tonight?"

"Don't know. Haven't thought about it. My old man's a jerk, and he's probably going to keep me on the phone for hours tonight asking me how I plan on paying for college or something. He owes me money, too. Hell, I inherited enough of the foolish shit from my mother. Why should I worry about it? Who needs to work when you have that kind of money?" He paused thoughtfully. "But then I don't get half the money until I'm twenty-one and that's a few damned years from now. Maybe I'd better work, huh? Anyway, I'll probably be having this same conversation with him tonight."

"Try not to let him upset you too much. It's not good for you." Penny could hear the solicitude in her voice, which made her sound too motherly. She couldn't let herself start mothering him. That would be disastrous! "Well," she said as he chomped at the bit, "if you call and I'm not here, keep trying." She felt her heart tear open and a tear beginning to form in the corner of each eye.

"Bye for now! See you later, Penny!" he said, and he was gone.

Naturally, he didn't take the elevator. She grinned through the tears she let escape; like any growing, healthy young male he tromped down the staircase two—three—steps at a time.

She closed the door, and the loneliness of the apartment closed in on her like a forbidding cloud.

That afternoon, she went downtown. Heightened by the sexual encounter, she felt like wandering through the streets of the Village and Soho. There were lots of interesting shops down there, and if she didn't dress in too matronly a style, she would feel quite free to go into any of them. She wore a pair of old jeans and her yellow cashmere sweater.

After a few hours of aimless wandering, she came across an interesting bookstore. In the window there was a book of erotic prints. She stood outside for a time, looking at it. And then it occurred to her. What a wonderful thing to buy for Robby. She was certain he had no idea that such things existed, had in fact existed for centuries. The page that this particular book opened to was from the Orient, showing a fat man fucking a woman from behind, her expression one of surprise.

Penny entered the shop and asked to see the book. The shopkeeper went to the window and withdrew it for her. It was of the finest quality, and thumbing through it, she noticed that it was a compilation of erotic pictures, not all having to do with the Orient. The most erotic, she found, were the French postcards showing women at the turn of the century, their skirts raised slightly, their breasts swelling over flimsy dresses. Robby would love it, she thought. There were a thousand lessons in those pictures. She bought it and returned home.

Once back in her apartment, she undressed with the intention of taking a bath. Setting her clothes on the bed, she saw her purchase lying there. She opened the pages randomly. Facing her was a picture of two women lying side-by-side, their thighs touching provocatively, though in seeming accident. One woman's hand touched the other's shoulder. Again remembering Kathryn, Penny got onto the bed and lay there, her finger moving to casually touch her cunt.

She turned the pages. There was a man standing with an erection, another man kneeling at his feet. Here again were two women. As she turned the pages, she worked her finger more vigorously around her clitoris. They were truly stimulating. In the back of her mind she thought of Kathryn, of Robby. Here was a girl with two men; here an older woman and a younger man. Penny focused on that picture, which was brightly colored and, she guessed, dated from the late 1800's judging by the clothing and overall modesty of the print. The woman's hand lay on the boy's thigh; it could have been a gesture of reprimand or invitation. She was obviously supposed to be his teacher. The boy's hand came up to her side, either to plead innocence, or to touch her breast. Penny touched her breast and thought of the night spent with Robby.

They were like these two people in the book. She was his teacher and he her student. The thought excited her, and she felt her body warm. There was, she thought, a faint shadow etched into the boy's crotch, implying an erection. Penny dipped two fingers into her cunt. She circled her forefinger around her now throbbing clitoris. Yes, she would teach Robby wonderful things.

She imagined him touching her breast in the same timid manner as was portrayed in the erotic print. She thought of the way he had sucked her, licked her, kissed her. She thought of his cock thrusting hungrily into her as, most definitely, the boy's cock would do to the older woman in the picture. And as her thoughts brought more and more life to the two people laid open before her, her cunt warmed, her clitoris expanded and her body shuddered. Then she closed her eyes, unable to focus any longer on the book before her, and rubbed her clitoris spastically until she came, her legs coming up as she bore down on herself, knocking the book soundlessly to the side.

Before preparing a lonely dinner she soaked for quite a long time in the tub. She brooded. If she didn't satisfy young Robby's violent sexual urges before the week was out, there'd be no more Robby. That seemed almost certain.

Then while running the soap up and down the length of her legs, the thought of Kathryn returned to her. She lathered the soap between her thighs, feeling the slippery smoothness of it and remembered how it had felt to have her anus penetrated by the girl's fingers. Within seconds she was sliding the soap all over her body, lathering her wet skin. Her cunt warmed to the feeling of the soap slipping between her breasts. She rubbed it over her erect nipples and thought of how she would teach Robby to stick his finger into her asshole.

She rubbed more frantically then, moving her hand down to her cunt, running the soap over the surface of it. The warm water lapped over her breasts as if licking them, and despite her earlier pain, she was urging her clitoris to full expansion with the edge of the soap, her buttocks bouncing slightly on the bottom of the porcelain tub, the water forming small waves. She spread her legs to the edges of the tub and stuck two fingers into her cunt while rubbing her clitoris with her thumb. Kathryn had lain there with her finger in my asshole, she had fallen asleep like that, she thought, her cunt gaping open in preparation for the release, which came a second later, the image heavy in Penny's mind of Kathryn's finger held by her squeezing asshole. As she came, she melted into the warm water, her spasms endless, the waves lapping at her breasts, which floated on the surface of the water.

Exhausted, she lay back, her long hair dangling

into the water, floating on the surface like seaweed. And then the memory came back to her, something about which she had long forgotten. It had to do with Kathryn. It was the last week before graduation. Penny, having wondered why Kathryn had crawled into bed with her that night, had finally asked her. They were lying in the dark night, each in her own bed. Her voice had come out soft and apologetic. And Kathryn had said something about wanting to touch her again, not answering the question. Then Penny had heard the rustling of sheets and Kathryn's footfalls over the wooden floor. In an instant, Kathryn was in bed with her. Penny's body warmed to the memory.

They had fallen into an embrace, their breasts pressing together. They'd kissed. Their tongues had gone into each other's mouths. Kathryn's hands had explored Penny's body, traveling down the faint swell of her belly to her thighs. Scared but aroused, Penny had spread her legs, and Kathryn had inserted a finger into her cunt. How much she had seemed to know about her pleasure; she'd rubbed her clitoris very softly, and Penny, mindless of everything except the new sensations in her body, had taken her hand to Kathryn's thighs. She'd felt the soft flesh of them, the dampness of her desire. She'd traced the outer folds of the girl's cunt.

Lying there, they had caressed one another's body for hours, it seemed. Then Kathryn rolled over so that she was lying prone on the bed. She asked Penny to lick her asshole, and Penny, somewhat disgusted with the thought but unwilling to let Kathryn go, began kissing along the girl's spine, causing Kathryn to arch her back and moan. At her buttocks, Penny had run her nose along the dark crevice, her tongue coming tentatively out to dab at the hole. Kathryn spread her legs and moaned, her finger reaching beneath her to tease her cunt. Penny hadn't understood this particular pleasure, but had continued to dart her tongue in and out of the girl's asshole while she brought herself to orgasm. Then afterwards, Kathryn had inched herself down Penny's now supine body and had begun to lick her cunt.

She'd stretched her tongue along the surface of it, so that the tip had reached nearly to Penny's asshole. That had felt wonderful and Penny had bent her legs and raised her buttocks into the air. Then Kathryn had dipped her head deeper into the dark space between Penny's thighs, her tongue stretching all the way to Penny's asshole, and had licked wildly. Penny, rubbing her clitoris, had been overwhelmed by the combination of sensations; her asshole had expanded, and Kathryn had stuck her firm tongue deep into it while Penny urged herself to orgasm, coming in powerful spasms, her buttocks clenching the girl's tongue tightly between them.

Penny sighed at the memory. Yes, she would have to teach Robby how to lick her asshole. She wanted his prick to penetrate her dark passage. Thinking about it, she reached her finger beneath her, the water growing colder, and ran it around the edges of her puckered asshole. Then she stopped. Later, she thought, emerging tired from the cold water.

At ten o'clock the grandfather clock began its mournful tolling, and by the time five gongs had pealed she was out the door on her way to Pete's Tavern. Perhaps Robby would show up after all.

Chapter Ten

Good evening to you, Mrs. Luckner," Bob grinned as Penny seated herself at the bar. It was Bob's immediate impression that she was full of mischief tonight; her eyes were twinkling, and a complete change had come over her. She had gone from a silent, brooding woman of questionable age to a seemingly young girl-about-town, anxious and ready for the night to unfold its secrets to her.

He prepared her drink and set it before her. Then he presented her wrapped-up cigarette holder. "For you, m'lady," he drawled cordially. She thanked him and apologized for being scatterbrained.

Bob had been reading a newspaper, and he returned to it. The inactivity in the bar made Penny think that Robby wouldn't be coming in. Of course there was no logical connection between the two, but Penny didn't see this; there was no room for logic in her emotions. Maybe he'd already been in and she'd missed him.

Despair overwhelmed her. She finished her first drink quickly, caught Bob's eye and soon had another, of which she swallowed half before lighting a cigarette nervously. As if to taunt her, her pussy began to ache. She felt a slight twinge in her clitoris, and when she crossed her right arm to flick the cigarette ash, her wrist accidentally brushed across her full breasts. The slight, momentary contact, coupled with her desire for Robby's cock, caused her nipples to rise.

The erotic torment continued. Once more, her eyes began to burn. Her breasts felt as if they were beginning to swell, and she couldn't resist pressing her thighs together to feel the slight pressure this brought to her clitoris. A rapid series of subtle internal explosions made her shiver slightly, and she bit her lower lip to suppress the sexual joy they promised.

She shrugged her shoulders. Oh well, she told herself, even if she didn't see him again, she had learned a remarkable lesson: she was simply bursting with sensual, erotic desire. She was in excellent sexual health, and the knowledge of this was comforting psychologically and gave her a great deal of personal relief, having feared lately that she was frigid.

As Bob handed her another drink she asked casually about the young man who had been in the night before.

"Oh, yeah, he came in for a quick drink. Seemed in better spirits tonight. He's got a way about him, that kid. He's got himself a good education, and that's something. Half the big words he uses ain't even in my vocabulary. Don't understand why his father's so disappointed in him. Of course, you never know the whole story."

Her heart slumped again, and the familiar sense of loss and uselessness, the clanging cymbals of an inferiority complex, began to sabotage her confidence. Fuck it! she said to herself. She'd have another drink and go back home. But first she'd ask Bob to give the boy her regards should he come in again. Perhaps Robby would remember to call her then.

She had her drink and, as she swallowed the last of it, said casually, "Tell the boy when he comes in again that I said good luck with everything." She wanted to say more, to slip in something by which Robby could not help remembering that he'd promised to call, but she didn't dare. Bob told her he'd pass the message along, and she slid his tip toward him and left.

Later, sitting in a hot tub again, she read the newspaper. She thought. She frowned. So little news, and pages of foolish advertising. She noted its fantastic circulation and dwelt a moment on the fleeting thought that if this were all the news its readership was fed, three-quarters of the population of New York must be absolute dullards.

In the kitchen, she made herself a double scotch. Then she sat naked on the couch in the very spot where Robby had brought her to such otherworldly heights of pleasure. She became resigned to the belief that he wasn't going to telephone her, that he was either asleep or busy with his friend from school.

Using the remote control, she turned on the radio and listened to the end of a symphony. It didn't satisfy her. She turned it off, and the telephone rang!

The grandfather clock began readying itself to strike twelve. She could hear the ancient mechanism grinding as she went to the phone.

"Hello, Penny? It's me."

"Well, hello there, Robby. You surprise me."

"It's not too late to call, is it? I hope not. I'm sorry if it is."

"No, Robby, no, it's not too late." Her knees felt wobbly. Her spine began to tingle as she listened to him breathing heavily into the mouthpiece. She recalled the feeling of his warm breath on her thighs, of his throbbing cock pounding into her.

"I've a favor to ask, Penny. It's quite serious, and I hope you'll understand. It's not money, so don't get scared."

She laughed. "What is it then, Robby?"

"Well, it's like this. You remember my friend, the one from school, Richie, the pal who returned the books?"

"Yes."

"Well, Penny, well, we got to talking, see, and I was feeling pretty important, if you know what I mean and…and I told him about you."

"So, you told him about me. Then what?"

"He doesn't believe me."

"So?"

He sighed. "Well, Penny, if you're not too tired,

could you do me this favor? It would really help me, because if I don't produce, Richie here is going to think I'm a liar—which I'm not, as you know—and that bother me, I don't know why, maybe because he's my only real friend fron school; and you know, it's not really worth all that, and I'm sorry I ever opened my mouth. But this ego thing...I'm sure being older and adult like you are, you know all about it, you know, my peers and things like that..."

Penny was amused.

"Then you want me to meet him, just so you can show him I'm for real. Is that it, Robby?"

He sighed deeply. "Yes, Penny."

She heard a jumble of voices—or was it just two voices? Robby's hand covering the mouthpiece made it difficult for her to hear. She pondered this. "Where would you like me to meet this Richie? Here in my apartment?"

"No, nothing like that. Could you throw something on, you know, like that yellow sweater and those white shorts and maybe those high heels, and come to the park? We'll be there...in the same place where we met...smoking. Richie brought some good grass."

Oh, Lord, grass! Penny thought, but she said over the phone, "Okay, I guess. When?"

"Then you'll come...tonight?" He sounded ecstatic. Her heart began to pump wildly and she felt a throbbing sensation deep up her pussy. The ache was subsiding slowly and being replaced by a quiet, subtle rumbling.

"Yes. Yes, Robby, as soon as I can, darling," she murmured, swallowing the word "darling" so he wouldn't hear.

"Penny," he was whispering, which meant Richie was close to the phone, "Penny? Maybe after he meets you and takes off, we can, well...you know, for a little while, huh?"

She almost collapsed. Her nipples began to harden

94

again. "Yes, yes, Robby. If you want to." She was overjoyed at his initiative and could hardly contain herself. She felt like shouting, but instead she simply hung up the telephone after telling her young lover she'd be coming as soon as possible.

She sprayed her deliciously nude body with yet another fragrance, and then slipped on the yellow cashmere sweater, without a bra, and the shorts, which were yellow to match the sweater. She wore nothing under them. This pair was even tighter in the crotch than the white ones, and a good quarter of her rounded, full buttocks was revealed to her appraising eyes. With the high-heeled, toeless shoes on her bare feet, she looked positively salacious, her long hair flowing softly onto her shoulders. She left the two top buttons of the sweater open, her breasts swelling alluringly, the outline of her dark nipples clearly visible. Throwing a raincoat over her shoulder, she took the elevator down.

"Think I'll enjoy a last cigarette in the park, Thomas," she said to the night attendant, who looked at her strangely. "It's a lovely moonlit evening, isn't it?"

"Yes, ma'am," Thomas answered, "and you couldn't be smoking in a safer spot on earth than our little park," he said, stepping aside to let her out. He listened to the click of her high heels on the corridor floor and shook his head when she'd disappeared. "Some piece!" he mumbled to himself, and brushed his fingers over his crotch.

Penny entered the west gate and circled around until she saw the two boys smoking on the secluded bench. The three of them were alone in the park. The lights at the north entrance winked in a steady rhythm. Two squirrels chased each other. In the distance, on the far East Side of the city, fire sirens were screaming, the winds from the river blowing the noise to her ears.

"Here she comes," Robby breathed to his friend. "Look at that, isn't she the greatest?" Penny had taken off the raincoat once she was in the park. Her luscious breasts jiggling and bouncing, her naked legs shining through the dark night and her hair shimmering on her shoulders, she looked like a dream come true to young Robby. To Richie she looked even better, like a wet dream come alive. He could hardly believe his eyes. The click-clack of her high heels stirred up every phantom he'd ever encountered in his erotic fantasies. The marijuana he'd been smoking, which Robby had refused, had put him into a mood so serene that time was passing in ultra-slow motion.

"Hello, there," she greeted the boys. Both stood up.

"This is my pal from school, Richard Timberly White the Third!" He looked at Penny then. "And Richie, this is a neighbor of mine who also lives on the park. Mrs. Penny…Mrs. Penny…"

"Jones," Penny helped.

"Yes," said Robby. "Mrs. Penny Jones." It was important that she be a married woman. All the more exciting for Robby.

They shook hands. Penny noticed that Richie's palm was wet with perspiration.

The three chatted amiably for the length of a cigarette, Richie's eyes caressing Penny's bountiful, half-exposed breasts every chance he got. Penny saw the young man, who was a head shorter than Robby and not half as well built, occasionally rub his cock or readjust its position. When Richie offered his cigarette, Penny said she didn't smoke pot. They discussed this for the length of another smoke, and then Richie abruptly stood up and announced he was going to take a turn around the park to appreciate the New York environment, ecologically speaking, while under the stimulating influence of his costly Mexican pot.

Robby and Penny began to kiss hungrily the very moment Richie left. His eager fingers were inside her sweater, fondling her bare breasts and stroking her hardening nipples. Her tongue was deep inside his wet mouth, her lips sucking on his tongue, her teeth nibbling on it. Passion raged inside her pussy, which was already pulsating.

Her fingers found his stiff prick. He let her open his fly and reach in. He wasn't wearing any shorts. She moaned with joy as she cupped his balls and squeezed them; then her hand slid swiftly up and down his hard tool, her fingertips massaging the velvet head, feeling it already leaking silver droplets.

"I want to go to the moon with you tonight, Penny. I want to suck you, your beautiful cunt. I want you to ask me...ask me, Penny!"

"Oh, darling," she breathed, pressing close against him, "I want to go to the moon with you. I want you to suck...to suck and lick...to suck my cunt...my wet cunt...my hot pussy, Robby."

His prick throbbed in her fist. He was breathing into her mouth, their tongues weaving, each taking a turn sucking voraciously on the other. Robby squeezed her breasts and pinched her nipples until Penny was groaning and whimpering, jerking his penis wildly, overwhelmed with ecstasy and hot passion as her pussy vibrated inside the extra-tight crotch of her scandalously brief shorts.

"Penny, oh, Penny...would you do me another big favor? Please...please?"

"Anything, Robby, darling, anything you want. I'll do it for you, baby...I'll fuck you, darling. I want you to fuck me. If you fuck me with your darling prick, oh, I adore your prick, darling...if you fuck me, I'll do anything." She was breathing rapidly. She was melting in his arms. He had opened her sweater to the waist and now he was kissing her erect nipples while his fingers stroked and fondled her precious breasts.

"What is it, Robby? What is the favor you want me to do for you? Tell me."

"Would you let Richie, my pal, watch us when I suck your hot cunt?" he asked solemnly, without looking up.

Chapter Eleven

Penny was truly shocked and pulled away from him abruptly. He pulled her back, nuzzling between her warm breasts, wetting the silky globes with his tongue, feeling her warm body writhe against his lips. "You said you'd do anything I asked, Penny," he whispered, his eyes searching through the darkness for Richie, who was then making the last turn, his hunger for what Robby had half-promised almost eating him alive.

"Yes, yes, I did, darling, but..."

"It would be a fantastic favor, Penny. You see, he now believes that you exist, but he still doesn't believe that I sucked you. You see," he kept whispering, "the boys up at school said they'd done everything. They're always bragging and telling lies. But me, I'm different. When I say I'm a virgin, I am one. And when I told Richie—he's coming now—that I'd sucked your pussy and you let me to, and when I told him that you sucked my prick and you wanted to and you liked it so much—well, he called me a liar!"

"Oh, Robby, you shouldn't have said anything. What will he think of me?"

"I wouldn't worry too much about that, Penny. He's a closed-mouthed kid, good family—like mine—and he's trustworthy. We roomed together. We tell each other everything, but he doesn't believe me about you. He said so."

Penny was silent for a moment or two. "Where would we...where would we, ah, demonstrate this...this, what you want me to do, Robby?" she asked seriously, a tiny fear beginning to fester in her stomach.

"I have it planned," he said. "See that old shack, the park-keeper's little house over there? Well, it's

99

always open because no one who comes to the park, except maybe a young kid, would take anything. Inside there's a single bed and an easy chair the old man uses. He lives in the Bronx, and there'd be no one to know we were in there. It's dark, too, so Richie wouldn't be seeing too much, you understand, and he'd maybe just hear you moaning a little, and he'd believe me then. You wouldn't even have to get undressed, just let me pull your panties down to your knees. You could sit in the easy chair where the old man smokes."

"Oh, Robby, yes. Yes, darling, I guess it would be all right...if we do it that way. I guess there's no real harm, is there? We won't get caught or anything."

"No, Penny. Never! Never!" He was breathing rapidly, his young body heaving. "Would you? Would you, please, Penny? It'd be the greatest favor ever, and I'll make it up to you. I promise."

She returned her hand to his cock. It was softening. Deep in thought, she absently played with it, rubbing the length of it, brushing his tender balls with her fingertips. Was she getting herself into something that could get out of hand? She had a sneaking suspicion that this coup had been planned as a great, impossible dare.

"No one will disturb us, right? And no one can see in? And it's dark in there, right, Robby?"

"Yes." His eyes searched hers, begging, pleading. He was holding his breath. His cock was shriveling up in her fist.

"And we won't take long...before your friend leaves, I mean, Robby?"

"No."

"All right, then," she smiled and kissed his mouth. "All right, darling, I'd love to do you the favor!" It was important to her that he relax now so that she could fondle and stroke his prick back to its magnificent hardness.

Richie returned at that precise moment. If the scheme had been planned, Penny thought, quickly releasing her hand and closing her open sweater, the boys' timing was as perfect as that of a commander in battle. Despite herself, she was amused. And despite her earlier misgivings, she felt a wave of excitement surge through her body. She listened as Robby, standing and zipping up his fly, whispered to Richie. Penny saw Richie's eyes light up, the surprise in them seeming genuine enough to indicate that this whole business was spontaneous indeed. When Penny stared at the young man, Richie averted his eyes, apparently quite embarrassed that Robby would go to such extremes to prove his personal integrity.

But what did it really matter? she thought as the three of them cut across the path, then over the thick grass to the little house in the middle of the park. It was surrounded by tall old trees and looked very much like the setting of a chidren's tale from a story-book, secluded and mysterious and yet, at the same time, friendly.

As Robby had said, the door was open. "I've got a little surprise, Penny," he said in a soft voice.

She had to laugh when he reached next to the comfortable easy chair and produced a bottle of sherry and three glasses. Ah, so it *had* been planned! Three glasses! Well, she was all the more amused and somewhat impressed with Robby's cunning. He had really fooled her. She must, she thought, remember this talent he possessed. She laughed and hugged him, kissing his mouth.

What the hell! she thought, watching Robby unscrew the cork. Why not be a part of it? Besides, she couldn't deny the intense thrills surging through her body at the thought of exhibiting her pleasure, her cunt, to a total stranger.

She sat easily in the big chair. The small room smelled of tobacco. The keeper smoked pipes; a tray of them rested on an end table. Robby, again sampling the wine, poured her glass first, Richie's next, and then his own. He almost spilled it, he was so nervous.

Richie took a position on the bed. Penny saw a blanket folded up at the foot of it. She also saw a sink and a toilet inside an enclosure. A two-burner electric stove sat on top of a small refrigerator. After he pulled the curtains closed, Robby lit a short, white candle, and soon its yellow flame was flickering in the magic darkness and the awe-inspiring silence in the middle of the park.

"We're perfectly safe, Penny," Robby assured her, sitting at her feet now, his glass of sherry in one hand, his other on her naked knee, his fingers slowly walking up toward her silky thigh.

Penny turned to Richie. "Richie, have you ever seen two people make love? I mean, a young man like Robby and an older woman?"

"Oh, God, no!"

"You want to, though, don't you?"

"Oh, God, yes!"

"Are you excited, Richie? Is your cock getting hard?" she teased, rather enjoying herself now as she felt Robby's fingers caressing her crotch through her extremely tight shorts.

Richie mumbled something she didn't hear. "Richie, are you going to play with your prick while Robby and I make love right in front of your eyes?"

He mumbled again. He was bent over, his glass on the floor of the shack. The silence was terrifying. The candle was now burning soft blue and bright yellow. She could smell the wax. She sipped slowly from her glass; the sherry was very tasty. She let Robby spread her thighs apart and rub his fingers over her crotch. When his index finger grazed her clitoris, she let out a slow moan, exaggerating it a bit for Richie's pleasure.

"Richie," she said, "why don't you sit closer? You could see better..." She raised up and slid forward as Robby's fingers urged her to greater excess. Then she watched his beautiful, handsome face in the candle-light as he expertly unsnapped her tight shorts and slowly drew them down her thighs, exposing her dark nest of rich pussy hair.

Richie gasped. He moved to the end of the bed.

"Take your cock out if you want, Richie. Don't be embarrassed. You can take down your pants, too, if you wish." She stepped out of her shorts and was now stark naked from the waist down to her high heels. As she stood there, her long hair flowing about her shoulders, Richie's eyes almost popped out of his head. Never had he imagined any woman to be so beautiful!

"Richie, look, look up. I'm going to unbutton my sweater and let Robby take it off. You'd like to see my naked breasts, wouldn't you? Wouldn't you like to look at them and at my nipples?" She stood before him, as if daring him to touch her.

"Oh my God!" was all he breathed.

Penny was enjoying herself immensely now. Tossing the yellow sweater onto the bed, she thrust out her voluptuous breasts, her nipples as stiff as pebbles. When the candlelight fluttered, the shadows cast by her breasts were wild and enticing. Richie was afraid he'd come inside his pants.

She spun around and around on her high heels, feeling positively beautiful. The boys' eyes consumed her shimmering nakedness, fed on her rounded, naked buttocks, her pussy hair, her gleaming thighs, her long, naked legs and her petite toes.

Then she sat down in the easy chair. Robby, giving a knowing glance to Richie, kneeled in front of her, parted her thighs and began to kiss the inside of them. Penny raised one knee and braced her foot on the edge of the chair. Richie could see perfectly now.

He couldn't take his eyes from the pink line of her slit. Quickly, he opened his pants and stood, letting them fall to the floor. He kicked them off. Then he sat down on the floor close to his school friend. His cock, which was long and thin and capped with a rapidly swelling head, bobbed in the air, knocking against his belly.

"Robby, darling," Penny interrupted, "why don't you get undressed too. I think Richie would love that. Wouldn't you, Richie?" This was more arousing than she ever would have imagined. Her cunt was weeping now, and her body trembled as she stared hungrily at Robby, who stood and undressed quickly, his prick rock-hard. She leaned forward and kissed it, licking the tip, and Richie almost turned blue. She smiled at Richie, beckoning him to stand. He did. Putting her arms around his small waist, she drew his short body closer to her. She lowered her face and brushed her lips across his erect cock, licking it tentatively, tasting it. Richie had a fine prick, strong and long, but not as handsome as Robby's.

"Now," she said, stretching and then cupping her breasts, "the performance will begin!" She looked up at Richie, who was standing as stiff as a statue, his eyes fluttering, his hands not knowing what to do with themselves. Penny solved that. "Richie, hold your nice cock with one hand, the hand you always use, and come closer and play with my breasts while Robby does me with his tongue, okay?"

"I guess so," Richie stuttered. As his hand found one of her warm, large breasts, Robby's tongue flickered, inching up inside her pussy lips, coming closer and closer to the center of her passion.

Chapter Twelve

At first Richie touched her breast tentatively, as if apologizing to it, but as Robby's tongue delved deeper and deeper into her cunt, she laid her hand over Richie's and told him to touch her however he wanted to. As if to stress her point, she squeezed her hand over his, thus squeezing her breast. Richie moaned and fumbled with his cock inexpertly, overwhelmed by the feel of her soft, full flesh.

Robby, kneeling before her, put his own hand to his cock, pressing it against her calf as he licked her cunt. Looking up momentarily, he saw his friend standing above him, cock in hand, touching Penny's breasts. A momentary twinge of possessive jealousy swept over him, but then he remembered that it had been his idea and that, therefore, he had no right to be jealous. Instead, he slid his tongue up and down her outer folds, thankful that she had complied.

To her side, Penny could see the boy's cock. It seemed awkward in his hand, as if he'd never touched it before. His finger moved around and around her hardened nipple, making it numb. She gently lifted it away and placed it on her other breast. Then she grasped his cock with her hand and squeezed it hard. The boy moaned from deep within his throat, causing Penny to shudder from the primordial sound of it. Stroking his cock now, she crossed her arm over her body and squeezed his tight balls in her palm. In this position, his arm was locked against her body, pressed to her breasts.

How was he going to keep from coming? Richie wondered. He couldn't just explode onto her right then and there. That would make him seem too young, too inexperienced. Instead, he concentrated on the wall behind Penny, studying it in order to momentarily forget his pleasure. The wall was hard, dark. Her hand squeezed his cock, sending waves of warmth rushing through his body. Hard, dark, hard, dark, he thought. Robby stabbed his tongue into Penny's gaping cunt, licking up her wetness, tasting her sweetness. He lapped at the edges of it, pushing the folds into the center where, it seemed, they got sucked in.

Soon Penny began to moan in earnest, her head swaying from side to side. She had dropped Richie's balls and was now merely holding his cock, squeezing it, jerking it up and down rapidly in time to the increased surging within her cunt. Her other hand went to the top of Robby's head, forcing it harder against her now throbbing cunt. Richie, forgetting the wall, looked down at his friend. Robby's head bobbed on Penny's white, translucent thighs, and Richie could see his tongue darting in and out like flames, the thin thread of her desire strung from her cunt to the tip of Robby's tongue. He could see her buttocks rising off the seat of the chair, her fingers digging into Robby's scalp, forcing him against her cunt.

Without thinking, without caring whether she would mind or not, Richie bent down and took one of Penny's breasts into his mouth, wrapping his lips firmly around her erect nipple. He sucked hard, his tongue sweeping over the expanse of swollen flesh, his teeth biting gently down. Robby glanced up Penny's body to see Richie's tongue spiraling around her nipple. A surge of agonizing desire passed through his cock, making it leap into the air. He pressed it harder to her calf. For some reason, he wanted Richie sucking his cock more than anything else.

He reached up and took Penny's breast into his hand, squeezing it, his fingers brushing against Richie's lips and cheek. This was too much for Penny, who began to writhe on the chair, to moan, to thrust her hips against Robby's face. She could feel the beginning pulsations in Richie's cock, the blue vein, which ran the underside of it, urging itself into her fingers. Robby speared his tongue deep inside her cunt, whipping it back and forth, straining to reach the back wall and up into her womb. His finger massaged and caressed her breast, his thumb pushing her nipple into the yielding flesh and then pulling it out, stretching it away from her, causing her to groan in agony.

She gripped Richie's cock roughly, tugging at it, urging it to explode. Her fingers dropped to his balls and tickled them. Richie's mouth gripped her breasts, wetting them, sucking them into his throat. He was going to come. He began to pump his cock into her fist, his buttocks expanding and contracting in the effort, his swollen head poking through the circular opening made by her enclosing fingers.

Feeling Richie's cock expand in her hands, she ground her wet cunt into her young lover's face, her clitoris rolling around on his tongue. She arched her back and pumped her fist furiously up and down the other boy's cock. Robby took his own cock into his hand, unable to stand it any longer. He squeezed it, he pushed it hard against her strong leg. All at once, their passion exploded, as if timed perfectly to one another.

Richie's fluid shot out onto Penny's breast while she writhed against Robby's face. Robby, feeling Richie's tongue slide over to his fingers on Penny's breast, rubbed his own cock, his pleasure exploding onto Penny's leg. There was a collective shudder, one that passed from Robby's cock to his tongue to Penny's cunt to her hand and finally to Richie's overjoyed cock, and then they fell away from one another, sated for the moment and exhausted.

"That was beautiful," she breathed. "So very beautiful!"

Robby sat quietly on the floor. Richie sat down next to him. Penny opened her eyes finally and saw that both boys still had handsome erections. Robby's prick was indeed an inch or so longer than Richie's. They were staring at her relaxed body as though she were a specimen of some kind. She grinned and spread open her thighs so they could clearly see the finest details of her cunt, open and exposed and glistening now from Robby's abundant saliva mixed with her own creamy juices, seeping from her open hole and running down her thighs. Her pussy hair was in disarray, and she used her fingers to comb it out, making both youthful pricks bob and jerk all over again.

She ran three fingers between her wet, purplish lips and then brought them up to her mouth. Looking intently at the boys, she licked them clean. The sight of this vulgarity pleased them, and their eyes brightened. She did it again. They sat closer, staring. She felt like an animal in a children's zoo. Then she inserted three fingers deep inside her cunt, moaning as she did, and they both licked their lips. She repeated this action and sucked her fingers clean, weaving and whipping her tongue over them before taking them fully into her warm mouth.

Penny was delirious with passion. Her pussy throbbed and pulsed. Her juices were still flowing, her thighs moistened by them.

She sat up and took her glass to her mouth, draining it. She held it out to Robby, and he filled it quickly. She drained it again, and again held it out to him. The warmth of the strong wine made her feel good, and she no longer cared if she got drunk. Her head was swimming delightfully. The candle seemed like two candles, the boys' beautiful cocks like four lovely instruments of sheer passion. She felt so comfortable and so relaxed, her naked body stretched out, her breasts heaving provocatively as she breathed in and out, her fingers still playing casually with her pussy. With the boys' eyes fixed hungrily on her cunt, she made her fingers vanish between the glistening lips and then, after a time, reappear. Then she took them slowly to her nipples, smearing her creamy juices around the dark brown flesh of them, causing them to harden even more.

"Play with yourselves," she said in a soft whisper. "I want to watch you jerk off, and then I want you both to do me a little favor."

They nodded their heads in unison, their lips parting in desire. Each took hold of his penis and began to pump it. Penny stared, licking her lips. How this scene excited her! She felt a new kind of trembling now. Richie sat cross-legged while Robby's legs were splayed out before him. Both of their cocks rose straight and hard into the air. They manipulated them with perfect knowledge of their pleasure. Richie pumped his hard, his tight fist moving up and down the length of it. Robby bore down on the base of his as he rubbed his saliva-wetted palm over the swollen head.

"I want you to play with each other," she said, again whispering softly, and the boys turned to look at each other, smiling. Robby shared his wine with his buddy and then placed the glass on the floor.

They sat closer to one another, shifting their bodies so that Robby's legs ran along the outside of Richie's, their cocks coming out from what seemed to be one lap. Penny sat above them, their bodies in profile. Each took a hold of the other's cock, closing their fists around them, and began immediately to pump up and down. Penny seethed with renewed passion. This had always been a fantasy, to watch two men please one another.

She watched as Richie's fingers unwound themselves and curled again around Robby's cock. He had done that for her benefit, knowing from the sound emanating from her throat that it had aroused her to see him taking the boy's cock into his hand for the first time.

As they were not at all bashful, they seemed quite experienced. It was apparent that this was not their first time indulging one another. Robby's hand traveled lightly, teasingly, up and down Richie's enflamed cock, his fingers scissored to trace the outline of it. When he reached the tip, he rubbed his palm over it, spreading the small droplet of escaping sperm around and around the purple bulb. Richie moaned and shifted his buttocks on the floor, clenching them and relaxing them alternately.

Richie was less deliberate, simply jerking his hand up and down Robby's cock, squeezing it hard as he did so. This seemed to give Robby the most pleasure, for his eyes closed and he too began to squeeze his friend's cock. Both cocks seemed to expand. As Robby bore down on the base of Richie's cock, rubbing his palm all the while over the bulb of it, Richie began to pump himself into Robby's fist, on the verge, it seemed, of coming. Robby pulled his hand away, telling him softly to be patient. Meanwhile, Penny began to touch herself, unable to help it. Nothing was as thrilling as seeing the two boys' hands working each other's pleasure so expertly.

"Have you ever blown each other?"

The thought of this fired her imagination even as it ran against her moral grain. But this new sexual abandon she was experiencing allowed her forbidden thoughts to tease her sensual curiosity. She was certain the boys' answer would be in the affirmative. Well, she would encourage them just this once, and after this adventure, she would guide them securely onto the path of heterosexuality, thus assuring her body and her conscience of total satisfaction.

Robby's eyes were glassy. He took a long swallow

from the wine glass and nodded somberly. The memory was sublime.

"You, Richie? Have you ever sucked Robby's prick?"

"Yes. Yes."

"Do you like sucking his prick, Richie?"

He nodded.

"Let me watch you blow Robby, let me see your lips on his prick. Let me see how you take his cock into your mouth and suck on it, Richie." Her voice was so lazy and so soft and so seductive that both boys seemed hypnotized by the sound of it.

"Come up here and sit on the arm of the chair, Robby, and kiss my mouth while Richie sucks on your pretty cock, darling. I want you to play with my nipples, and I want to kiss you and play with your balls while your friend kisses your beautiful prick and sucks on it. I want to see him up close. I want to watch your prick go in and out of his mouth, and I want my tongue in your mouth and your hot balls in my hand, Robby."

There was an atmosphere of unreality in the cabin. The flickering candle, the profound silence—only now and then a distant street noise intruded—the nearly empty wine glasses reflecting the sparkling light, the three of them, naked and eager...

Robby straddled the arm of the chair, his strong thighs spreading over it, his one foot resting on the seat next to Penny's thigh, his leg bent into the air, his other leg dangling down the other side. His cock stood up against his belly. She watched as Richie bent his head, his mouth opening as it neared the boy's cock. He set his lips upon it and slowly spread them over the swollen head, slipping it fully into his mouth. He began to suck, and Penny could see in the candlelight the shadows of his furrowed cheeks as he took Robby's cock to his throat. Robby leaned over and kissed Penny, their tongues entering one another's mouths in the same instant in which their lips met.

Reaching down to take Robby's balls into her cupped hand, Penny grazed Richie's face. His tongue came out and flicked across the underside of her wrist. He took her finger into his mouth and then, carrying it with him, took Robby's cock back in. For an exquisite moment, Penny felt the wet slickness of Robby's cock enclosed within the walls of Richie's mouth, her finger being sucked as wholly as the boy's cock. Then she pulled her finger away and began to tickle Robby's balls. Robby took his hand to Penny's breasts after licking his fingers and began to pinch her nipples and massage her full flesh.

"Do you want him to suck me until I come inside his mouth, Penny?" Robby asked, his breathing increasing as his friend's mouth sucked and slobbered up and down his vibrating shaft. "He likes that most of the time, don't you, Richie? Tell Penny how you like me to shoot off in your mouth."

Richie nodded, his eyes smiling as he kept up his rhythmic sucking.

Penny moaned when Robby squeezed her breasts hard in his palm and lowered his head to them. He took her nipple between his lips and began to bite down.

"I have other plans," she said, moaning, "other plans." He pulled his head away, and disappointment rushed through her. "Bite them, Robby, bite my breasts. It feels so good." His head fell eagerly back to her breasts, his open mouth ready to devour them.

Holding Robby's hot balls, Penny could feel Richie's saliva dribbling down the throbbing shaft, collecting at the base of the column. She rubbed this juice into his balls, then put her fingertips back to Richie's open lips, feeling his slippery tongue as it clung to Robby's cock and then disappeared back

112

into his mouth as he took the full length of the prick down his throat.

It was quite instructive to watch a man suck another man's cock. Similar lessons could be learned by a man watching a woman sucking another woman off, she thought, though Robby had done quite well with himself. She watched as Richie flicked his tongue over the head of Robby's cock and then squeezed it between two fingers. The resulting moan was deep and full of satisfaction. Then Richie bent the shaft all the way down and let it spring back up, catching it in his open mouth and sucking it between his lips in one fluid motion. The sounds of his slurping were maddeningly arousing to Penny.

"Robby, darling...I have a surprise for you." Having almost forgotten herself, so wrapped up was she watching the two friends making hot, forbidden love to each other, her heart began to pound as she remembered what she'd planned.

Before leaving the apartment, she had tucked a bottle of expensive, oily lubricant into her raincoat pocket. All the way to the park she had shivered, visualizing how she intended to use it...once Robby's friend had departed.

Her anus began to twitch at the thought.

Robby lifted his mouth from her breasts and nodded excitedly.

"You recall asking me if the penis ever missed the cunt hole and accidentally slid into the asshole?"

He raised his head. His eyes looked puzzled. "Yes."

"In a little while, darling, after I watch you suck on Richie's prick, do you think the two of you might try to miss my cunt on purpose?"

Chapter Thirteen

The puzzled, quizzical look remained in Robby's brown eyes. He wasn't at all sure he understood! She couldn't mean what she was suggesting! No, he couldn't believe that she wanted him to fuck her little asshole.

"You mean it?" he asked aloud. Richie, on the other hand, didn't understand at all. His eyes darted from the nest of Robby's cock, his mouth fully enclosed over it, and he pulled away. His mouth gaped open in his confusion, saliva wetting his lips so that they glistened in the candlelight. And then, getting no answer to his silent question, he leaned back down and swallowed the boy's cock again, happy to have it back in his mouth.

"I mean it, darling," she said, embracing him warmly. She kissed his neck and his ears, taking one of his ears into her mouth and worming her tongue inside it, making Robby quiver.

"Now, you get busy on Richie's prick. I'd love to see you sucking it. Besides, he's had enough of sucking yours, Robby. Now it's your turn to make him really hot and horny, but be careful. Don't make him come. I want his prick as hard as it is now." She kissed his mouth ravenously, and he climbed off the arm of the chair. "Come up here, Richie, and I'll kiss you like I kissed Robby. Think you'd like that?"

"I love it all. I'll do anything, I swear." He sighed and brushed his hand over his cock, which jerked in response. "I can't believe I'm here doing this. I can't believe how beautiful you are, your naked body, I mean. I can't believe I'm sucking Robby's cock while you watch." He crawled breathlessly to the arm of the chair, which had been warmed by Robby's buttocks. He, too, straddled it.

Penny put her naked arm around his shoulders and

drew his head down to her breasts, urging him to suck on them and to lick her nipples. She held the globes in her hands and guided them into his burning lips.

Robby took Richie's prick into his mouth, swallowing deeply, exhaling loudly. He worked his mouth expertly up and down the shining length of it, his tongue spiraling around it, digging into the folded rim of the head. Richie began to thrust his hips toward Robby's face while he gnawed on Penny's aching nipples. Her head was thrown back, her mouth open, her legs spread wide to her hand. She listened to the sounds of Robby's mouth on Richie's cock. He took it deep into his throat and twisted his tongue around the base, his breath warming the thick nest of the boy's pubic hairs.

Penny opened her eyes. Each time Richie's prick vanished into Robby's mouth, she felt a spear of delight penetrate her to the very core. He was an excellent cocksucker, judging by the undulating motions of Richie on the arm of the chair. Richie's widely spread legs thrust forward and were taut with tension. His balls spread outwards and clung to his inner thighs. Robby opened his jaws wide, letting Richie shove his cock deeper into his mouth, forcing it to the far wall of his open throat.

Though he could not admit it to himself, this was, to Robby, more arousing than anything at all, and he was anxious for things to go further, for he and Richie to suck one another at the same time. In the back of his mind hovered the idea of fucking Richie. But he couldn't let himself think about that. That was wrong, wasn't it? He ran his tongue over the boy's hot flesh and felt the surging of eroticism deep within his gut. It felt so good to have Richie's cock buried in his mouth, to give him pleasure.

His fingers scratched Richie's naked buttocks and gripped him, forcing his prick even deeper down his open throat.

Penny's pussy and asshole were both blazing now. Her whole body was sweating from the strong wine and the wild, erotic excitement. She was feeling dizzier as the minutes passed. She fingered her pussy while Richie cried out, his groin heaving, one blinding spasm following another as Robby sucked and sucked, licking around the head and down the shaft.

She sat forward, and when Robby's mouth pulled free of Richie's almost-bursting prick, she bent her head and took it deep into her mouth, emulating Robby's motions, teasing the head with her tongue tip, licking down to the balls, then letting her tongue flutter up to the head again before swallowing the length of the shaft. Richie was squirming and quivering as she held his balls and massaged them, moving her fingers rapidly as she'd seen Robby do.

"Oh! Oh!" Richie squealed, and quickly Penny pulled her mouth away, the corners of her lips leaking saliva.

"Don't come, oh, don't come, Richie!" she cried, slapping his face. The sudden shock of her hand across his cheek did the trick, and he was able to hold back. The very idea that a woman was sucking his prick and touching his balls had almost been all that was needed for him to shoot.

"Stand in front of me, both of you," she said after a moment. "I'm going to lick both your pricks at the same time. Would you boys like me to do that?"

They needed no urging. Facing each other, their cocks met. Penny took one in each hand, jerking them back and forth, rubbing the two heads together. They seemed to like that. Then she leaned down and let her wet tongue lick up and down both long staffs. Her mouth darted from one luscious head to the other, her tongue and lips caressing and stroking them.

"Now, Robby," she said, releasing their gleaming tools, "be a darling and get the little bottle that's in the pocket of my raincoat." She stood up and Richie put his arms around her waist. He leaned over to kiss her wonderfully naked breasts. She could feel his cock urging itself into her groin. He pushed hard against her as he rubbed his nose between her two breasts.

"Here," said Robby.

"Okay, now the reason I want you both to put your pricks up my asshole instead of in my cunt," she said, loving the sound of the words she was using and the expressions on the boys' faces, "is that my cunt's still a little sore from Robby fucking it last night."

Richie looked at Robby. "You didn't tell me that you screwed her, too!"

"You didn't even believe that she let me suck her pussy, did you? So who would expect a dumbshit like you to believe I fucked her?"

"Now never mind," said Penny. She was terribly anxious to see if what she'd planned was possible. She got down on the floor on her hands and knees. "Now, each of you take turns licking my behind, all of it, the little hole, too," she said, wiggling her deliciously naked buttocks in their faces as they kneeled in back of her. She lowered her chest, and her breasts rubbed against the rough wooden floor of the cabin. She felt her buttocks being spread open, her asshole exposed. She felt a kiss, then more kisses, and then the very tip of a tongue dive into her opening. A second tongue stroked her buttocks while the first worked pointedly at her anus. New emotions, quite unlike anything she'd expected, began to travel the length of her body, titillating her nipples and making her spine tingle. The tongue at her asshole was now two tongues, and one of the boys was spreading her buttocks so wide apart she thought she would break in two.

As Robby and Richie teased and licked her asshole, they touched tongues, entwining them around one another, alternately sticking them into Penny's hole. They kissed, their lips meeting at the entrance of her asshole, and then Robby dipped to between her thighs and kissed the surface of her cunt while Richie continued to circle his tongue around her ass, licking up and down the deep crevice separating her buttocks. His fingers grasped her, sinking into her flesh, making dark shadows there.

Penny rocked slowly back and forth, her nipples grazing the wooden floor as her asshole was filled by someone's wet tongue, her cunt licked. Her clitoris responded, beginning to sting and flutter.

She rotated her hips now, and her heart was palpitating as one tongue after another made her asshole simmer. The sensations were wild, wilder than when Kathryn had fingered her hole so long ago. The boys were now blowing hot air into her asshole, and an all-consuming desire for them flooded over her.

"Let me rest a minute, please," she exclaimed, and fell forward on the floor. Turning her head, she saw the two boys embracing and kissing one another, their tongues thrusting into each other's mouths, each straining to reach the back of the other's throat. They took one another's cocks into their hands again and began to jerk and pull at them in the same manner as before. Then, moving closer, they began to rub their erect pricks together, circling their hips slowly, pushing their cocks first to this side, then to that side. With their hands, they pressed them hard together, the swollen heads pushing into the soft flesh, pulsing hotly into it. Small droplets of clear fluid escaped from each tiny hole, and they smeared it around the heads with their fingertips, each boy massaging the other's now-moist cock.

"I think I'm ready now, dears," she said. She resumed her kneeling position, asking Robby for the blanket on the end of the bed so she could rest her face on it.

"Okay. Who wants to be the first to fuck me up the ass?" she laughed, feeling the wine coursing through her veins.

"I think Robby should go first, don't you, Robby?" said Richie. "After all, he's already screwed you and I'm still a virgin."

"Okay," answered Penny, "let him be the first. You see, no one's ever fucked my ass before, so I'm a virgin there, too."

Richie giggled at her dirty talk. He shoved Robby manfully. "Okay, you first, Mr. Breining."

"First, rub lots of oil over your cock, Robby. It's going to hurt me, I know. You've got such a big cock." Robby tipped the bottle over his palm and spread the warm, soothing oil over every inch of his prick. He could have come then.

"You think it'll fit, Penny?" he asked, encircling his palm over the swollen, slick head.

"It'll fit, darling. Don't worry, it'll fit."

Her asshole was already well-lubricated with the boys' saliva, so Penny's orifice seemed ready to accept anything.

"Is your entire prick well oiled?," Penny asked, having to laugh at her question. The whole scene seemed in a way ridiculous to her, but at the same time, it both terrified and excited her. Her ex-husband George should see her now; stark naked, down on her hands and knees, her long hair falling over her head, two naked teenagers about to fuck her asshole. George would probably drink himself to death in five minutes.

"Okay now, Robby, be extra careful until I tell you it's all right to put your prick in all the way. Take it easy, darling," she said, her breath coming fast, her heart pounding as she felt the head of his large prick touch her asshole. His hands closed around her hips.

It was Richie who positioned Robby's prick, aiming it, and slowly beginning to exert pressure. It wouldn't go in. Robby pushed his hips forward, and to his utter astonishment, it slipped in until the velvet head was covered. Penny moaned and began to move slowly, and this time the throbbing cock dipped in another inch. Penny felt as though she were being torn apart. She gritted her teeth. At the moment, she felt no excitement, no thrill whatever.

"A little more darling," she whispered. "A bit more, but slowly. It hurts."

"Shall I take it out, Penny?"

"Oh, no. Heavens no. Leave it in and just push a bit harder, but don't fuck me yet. Just push slowly and easily, and I know your prick's going to slip all the way up and then I'll love it! I know I will!"

Robby pushed again, but he couldn't force his prick in any deeper. As for Penny, the pain was increasing instead of diminishing, as she had hoped. Then she felt her sphincter muscle doing just the opposite of what she wanted. Robby's darling prick slipped out of her hot asshole. Looking back, she noticed he was losing his erection.

Penny sat up and faced them. "Oh, I'm so sorry, Robby and Richie. I guess it's not going to work. I think it's because we're all tired. That's probably it."

She was obviously disappointed. The boys saw this and both embraced her and kissed her face. Robby brushed her hair out of her face, and Richie fondled her breasts tenderly.

"I really am sorry. I was so looking forward to it myself, and I thought it would make the both of you so happy. Just think, you could have told your friends when you got back to school that you'd both fucked an older woman up her asshole."

The boys were silent, hugging and kissing and fondling her body. Both were now sucking on her breasts, and Penny held their heads, smiling.

"Is that rain I hear?" Penny interrupted their nursing.

"It's rain," Robby answered. "I know…let's all go out naked in the grass in front of the cabin."

"Will anyone see us, Robby?"

"Nope. No one. It's too dark."

She grabbed the wine bottle and drank from it. She passed it to Robby and Richie. They both swallowed deeply.

Penny was radiantly happy now. The moment she felt the cleansing rain, her heart leaped. She ran, her naked buttocks quivering. She lay down on her back in the grass. It felt positively wonderful!

The boys kneeled on either side of her, their erect pricks bobbing. She laughed happily and took them in her hands, tugging gently.

"I'm not going to let either of you go until you shoot your sperm all over me," she told them with mock seriousness. Then she began to pump them ferociously, pulling so hard that the boys had a hard time maintaining their balance on the slippery grass. "Let me see your cocks shoot onto me," Penny murmured. "I want you to drench me with your sperm." She tugged at them with long strokes, running her fist all along the length of their shafts and covering the swollen heads on the upstroke. The rain was falling more heavily now, wetting them all and exciting them to an even greater frenzy.

Penny pulled the boys closer together by their cocks. Now the heads were touching, burning hotly together. She raised her head abruptly and began to lick them with broad, slashing strokes. Both boys moaned as her warm, wet tongue darted back and forth from one cock to the other. Then she clasped one in each hand again, milking them, pulling on them, rubbing them together. She squeezed hard, the rain wetting their flesh, her palms sliding smoothly up and down the length of them. While her right hand moved up on Richie's cock, her left hand slid firmly down on Robby's.

Her arms were getting sore, and she rested them a moment, both hands now grasping the base of their cocks. It was Robby who, with his hand, forced the head of his cock against Richie's and began to rub it there, while Penny continued to bear down, squeezing hard. Soon, both boys were exploding, thick bursts of come dropping onto the heads of one another's cocks and Penny's hands and breasts. Penny continued to squeeze while the two boys rubbed furiously against one another. The rain washed everything away an instant after it landed.

A few minutes later, back in the cabin, Robby cleaned up. Penny rolled her clothes up in a ball and put on her raincoat.

The boys walked her to the gate, and they kissed good night, all three embracing.

"Robby, promise to phone me sometime this afternoon?" Penny asked, touching his lovely prick, still half-stiff.

"After we sleep, Richie and I have to fill out some stupid college application papers. That'll take a while, huh, Richie?"

"Yeah."

"Well," said Penny, suddenly feeling very drowsy, "remember to call when you finish, okay?"

"Penny," said Robby, after a moment's reflection, "maybe you'd like to come over to my house and help with the stupid forms?"

"I'd love to, Robby. I'd love to help you. I'll bring my portable typewriter."

"No, that's okay. We've got one."

Robby gave her the address. Penny, seeing no one around, kneeled on the wet sidewalk in the drizzling rain and took out both their pricks, sucking on them until they were rigid and pounding.

"Now, hurry home and suck each other off!" she squealed and, without looking back, darted across the street into her apartment building.

They ran triumphantly home to Robby's apartment across the way. Once there, anxious to follow Penny's instructions they fell into the foyer and immediately began to strip each other naked. It was Robby who pulled Richie onto the floor once unclothed. He couldn't wait.

In the dark, Richie climbed atop Robby's supine body and straddled it, taking his friend's cock directly into his mouth. He found Robby's open mouth with the tip of his own cock and drove it in. They pumped into one another's mouths, their buttocks working to push their cocks deeper in. Robby opened his throat and took the length of Richie's prick deep into it. Richie did the same, his forehead bearing down on Robby's thighs. This is what Robby had wanted to happen for so long, and he could hardly contain the outpouring of erotic joy.

He bore the weight of Richie's body easily, the boy's hips thrusting forward, sinking his cock deep into Robby's mouth. In a quick instant, Robby's hands came up and grasped Richie by the hips. He manipulated the boy then, pulling him down onto his face and pushing him off. Richie complied, his buttocks clenched and expanding as he lifted himself away so that the tip of his cock rested on the soft bed of Robby's lips. For his part, Richie kept hold of Robby's cock firmly, never letting it escape his mouth. Instead, he twisted his tongue around it, sliding it up and down until he felt Robby begin to expand, his buttocks now beginning to thrust upwards, his back arched. They came together, each boy's cock pulsing to the firm grip of the other's lips and the slippery movement of the other's tongue.

Afterwards, Richie rolled off Robby and turned his body so that they lay side by side. Casually and idly, they fondled one another's softening flesh as they talked about Penny, comparing their impressions of her. As their talk became more and more lewd, free then to use whatever words they wished to use, their cocks grew hard in each other's hands.

It turned into a kind of game to see who would shoot off first, using the most arousing language they could think of. Richie, holding firmly onto Robby's cock, squeezing it, said something about Penny's pussy being wet and pink, and Robby, likewise holding Richie's cock, told him how she tasted, describing in detail what he had done with his tongue and how her cunt had responded.

Their cocks throbbing in agonizing tension, they quit talking, for it was clear that no amount of dirty talk would make them come. They turned their heads and thrust their tongues into each other's mouths. Shifting their bodies, they turned to press against one another. They rubbed their cocks together, squeezing them as they did. With their mouths pressed together, their lips framing the darting motions of their tongues, they came again, this time wetting their thighs and their fingers, squeezing each other's cocks and forcing themselves hard against their pressing bodies.

Robby began to kiss down Richie's body. His brow pushing into the boy's stomach, he licked his release from the warm flesh, swooning to the feel of the boy's half-hard cock rubbing against his cheek. He wanted to fuck him, to fuck him like he would fuck a woman, like he'd fucked Penny. But he knew that wasn't possible, and frustrated, he pulled away. They got up slowly then and, gathering their clothes, went to Robby's bedroom, where they climbed naked into bed. But Robby, his desire enflaming his body, could not sleep. Hearing Richie's snores, he began to kiss him on the neck, feeling the tightness of it, pressing his lips to the stretched tendon there.

He moved down his body, kissing his nipples, biting them gently. Richie stirred. His cock, which had been lying placid between his thighs in his sleep, jerked to hardness, and yet Richie did not wake up. Robby moved to take it into his mouth, his own cock surging with new desire. How badly he wanted to turn Richie over and to fuck him in the ass. But he couldn't do that. Instead, he took Richie's cock wholly into his mouth and began to suck it hard. It grew to fill Robby's open mouth, and Richie slowly awoke, his body fully aroused.

In his state of dream-like wakefulness, Richie turned his body slowly around to take Robby's stiff cock into his mouth. Again, they began to suck on one another. Robby, moaning to the feel of complete enclosure, said something about wanting to touch Richie's asshole. But Richie, too sleepy to be aware of anything other than the warm pleasure in his loins, didn't hear. They pumped into one another's mouths, their bodies expanding, their surging passion infinite. They did not hear the front door being unlocked.

Chapter Fourteen

When Penny awoke at about noon, she felt very safe and wonderfully secure. She arched her naked body luxuriously, stretching every muscle. She felt happy, joyful. The bright noon sun outside her open bedroom window added to her enchantment. She let her hands caress her nakedness, rubbing her fingertips briskly over her stiffening nipples.

She cupped her hand over her crotch, loving the feel of her bushy pubic hair. She inserted one finger into her cunt, noting with interest that she was still wet from the night's activities.

Rolling onto her side, she stroked her buttocks and tentatively felt her asshole. It was very oily. Looking over her shoulder, she laughed when she saw a round grease spot on the sheet. What would Clara, the maid, think of that? She experimented with one finger, dipping it slowly into her greasy asshole. How easily it slipped in! It felt strange and good to her. She trembled and then tried to insert yet another finger, and this worked perfectly. She questioned why Robby had had so much trouble getting his prick in last night.

Oh, how much she'd wanted that! She knew now that the desire to be fucked anally had grown into an almost obsessive passion. The reason her muscles hadn't cooperated, she realized, was that she'd been nervous, unable to relax.

Climbing from bed, she picked up her hair brush. She studied it. The handle was round and almost, but not quite, as thick as Robby's prick. It certainly wasn't half as long, that was for sure! Grinning at her disheveled hair in the mirror, she fell back on the bed and, lying on her belly, gently inserted the handle of the brush into her rear channel. It fit smoothly, and her muscles did not reject it. She began to move it in and out slowly. Then, increasing the speed, she got onto her knees and pushed and pulled the brush in and out as deep as it would go.

Not a single pain! And she was enjoying the pressure. She reached back with one hand and played with her clitoris with her fingertips and soon she felt the ebb and flow of her passion flooding her mind and body as she increased the friction from the handle, her buttocks clenching around it. She felt buoyant, and the excruciating joy she was receiving was making her feverish. As her final spasm shot through her body, she pushed the handle as deep into her ass as it would go, clamped her thighs over her hand, and fell flat to the bed, letting go of the brush as she did.

"Really, there's nothing to it," she said aloud, and pulled out the handle with a soft plopping sound. She stood up, blew a kiss to her beautiful reflection in the mirror, and padded on bare feet to the bathroom. "Hello, Clara," she called toward the kitchen, as she entered the bath, leaving the door open.

"Good morning to you, Mrs. Luckner," came the sound of the familiar voice. Clara had been working for her ever since she'd married George.

While letting the shower thermostat adjust to the temperature she desired, she thought of the handle of the knife sharpener in the kitchen drawer. Her eyes brightened. If anything, this instrument was even larger and longer than Robby's cock. Reflecting on it, she decided that the circumference was about the same, and even the rounded knob on the tip of it was about equal to the velvet head of Robby's darling prick.

She had seen Clara pass by and heard her now in the bedroom. Quickly, she darted into the kitchen and rushed back with the knife sharpener. She closed and locked the door. It wasn't unlike Clara to walk in even when she was sitting on the toilet with the door closed. It would just never do to let Clara see what she had in mind to do with the instrument she held in her hand.

She adjusted the three-way mirror so that she could see the reflection of her white, rounded buttocks as she kneeled on the bathroom floor. She wondered why she'd not had the idea of using this before—up her pussy when she'd been so terribly frustrated in the past. But she dismissed the thought and, watching her reflection, saw the knob on the handle press against her asshole and then begin to penetrate it. There was some pain, but it didn't deter her. The pain even felt good as the staff of the handle sank deeper. She spread her thighs farther apart. Still watching the fascinating scene, and enjoying the pleasure-pain sensations immensely, she began to work the instrument further in. Then she pulled it almost all the way out and pushed it slowly back in. She worked it more vigorously then, finally setting a rhythmic pace that soon had her body vibrating and her hips rotating.

Already she could feel her juices gathering inside her pussy. She pinched her clitoris and a gigantic spasm shot through her body. *Ah yes*, she sighed to herself, halting the motion of the handle to watch it grotesquely protruding from her rounded buttocks, the sight amusing her and making her giggle. Yes! Yes! It worked!

Pulling it out, she measured the length of the handle that had been up her ass against the height indicator on the bathroom scale. Christ! she exhaled, almost six and a half inches! Curious now, she lay on her back on the floor and inserted the greasy handle into her pussy. Then, pulling it out, she measured it at seven and a half inches. Ah, so her asshole capacity was just one inch less than that of her pussy! As isolated facts went, this was interesting news.

Happy and impressed with her new discovery,

129

Penny rushed naked to the telephone in the living room. Directory assistance gave her Robby's number. She dialed it. It was answered on the second ring, and she recognized her young lover's voice. How like a mature man he sounded!

"Robby, this is Penny."

"Jesus, do we need you, Penny. We're in all kinds of trouble!"

"What trouble?" Her heart leaped! Had it something to do with the park?

"My stupid father came home unexpectedly in the middle of the night and caught Richie and me right in the thick of it. His cock was in my mouth, and mine was in his, and we didn't hear my father at all. The rotten, no-good sneak spied on us for minutes before we got wise!"

"Then what?"

"He whipped the shit out of both of us with his belt, that's what! And I'm running away, that's what else!" he said, the determination in his young voice striking a new fear in Penny's belly.

"Wait a minute…wait a minute, darling. Does he know anything about me?"

"Oh, God, no! If he did, he'd kill us."

Penny relaxed, exhaling deeply. "Listen, Robby…"

"And probably you too, Penny," Robby interrupted.

"Listen to me, Robby, just listen. Where is your father now?"

"Probably down at Pete's. He goes there because it's close. He's like a mad bull. Christ, what he didn't call us! He's even threatened to pull me out of school and send me to jail. But he can't do that. My schooling's all paid for. My mother did that."

"Robby, he's at Pete's now, right? Listen, let me do something about this. I'm sure I can. I don't know just what, but I'll think of something. Your little moonmaid's not a dumb bunny."

130

He laughed. "I know that. Really, Penny, you'll try something…to fix it up? Like what? I can't think of anything," he said wearily. "Nothing. Richie's scared to death my father's going to tell his father. He promised to. They know each other pretty well."

"Robby, I'll leave word with the doorman at my place to let the two of you into my apartment. You both come over here now. I'm going to dress and go down to Pete's. Stay here until you hear from me, understand?" Penny felt a curious strength simmering in her body. She felt strangely protective. And oddly enough, she had no fear of what she felt she had to do. This wasn't at all like her, to walk where angels feared to tread, but that was precisely what she was going to do!

She hung up when Robby agreed to her plan. She showered quickly and dressed as sexily as possible, slipping on a pale lavender sweater, which clung tightly to her swollen breasts, her nipples rising clearly against the soft fabric. She put on a very short wraparound skirt of a deeper shade of lavender. This allowed her long, shapely legs to be exposed almost up to her deliciously curved buttocks. She knew that if she so much as leaned over, her naked behind would be revealed. Slipping a new pair of leather sandals on her feet, she brushed out her hair. Pleased with the results, she hurried out the door, down the elevator, around the park, and down Irving Place. Nearing Pete's Tavern, she finally slowed down, her walk becoming seductive. Casually, she entered the bar.

Chapter Fifteen

Robert Frederick Breining, Sr. who at fifty years of age was graying at the temples, had thoughtful, brown eyes, particularly handsome features, a strong, well-exercised body and long, sensitive fingers, sat now in a darkened booth in Pete's Tavern. Before him on the table were two glasses, one empty and one half-full.

The bustling luncheon crowd usually associated with Pete's at that time of the day was either skipping lunch or eating elsewhere in the quiet neighborhood. No one sat at the bar. The booths on either side of him were empty. The television set in the corner was on, but the sound had been turned off. Bob the bartender, working the swing shift for the balance of the week, was pouring the dregs from nearly empty bottles into others containing more booze. He thought more than once, as he glanced over at the lone gentleman sitting in the most secluded of the booths, how close a resemblance he bore to the young man he'd met two nights ago.

Yes, the brooding gentleman looked so much like the kid, the kid could have easily been his son.

He heard the door open and glanced up. His eyes practically popped from his head. It was Mrs. Luckner. Christ, he breathed, what was she up to? Her costume was fantastic. He felt his prick jolt when he saw her flashing, naked thighs and her lovely, full breasts bouncing and quivering under her tight sweater. What the hell had gotten into her? he wondered. It was the difference between day and night! She was all smiles.

"What are you doing here at this hour?" she asked brightly, her eyes exploring the bar, spotting and recognizing Robby's father instantly. There was no question. That was just how Robby was going to look when he was older. How handsome!

Bob explained the swing shift and then gave her a scotch. "And how about you, Mrs. Luckner? How come you're here this time of day—if it's any of my business?" he grinned. He found it hard to keep from staring at her nipples. The sweater was so tight she might just as well have been naked; every lovely curve of her ripe, perfectly molded breasts was visible.

"I feel good, Bob. I'm out of the doldrums...at last."

Bob looked over her shoulder. The gentleman in the booth had swallowed the balance of his drink. "Another one, sir?" Bob asked.

Robert Breining looked up. "Yes. Make it a double, if you please." Then he stood up, carrying the two empty glasses. He stood at the bar waiting for Bob to fix the drink.

"Sit down, sir, I'll bring it over to you," said Bob amiably.

"No, that's fine. I think I'll drink it right here and be off." He was standing a seat away from Penny. They caught each other's eye and she smiled. He nodded and looked as though he wanted to reciprocate, but didn't.

Penny was fascinated with his face. Every single feature was reproduced in his son's, even his cute ears. She felt a slight tremor pass through her when she glanced down at his lower body, much in the same way she remembered appraising Robby when he had stood to leave that first night.

She had begun to wonder about the size of his cock and his skill in bed when she felt his eyes on her breasts. She turned and looked at him. She smiled again. She had to take the plunge quickly; he looked as though he were planning to leave. But he spoke first.

"I've seen you in the neighborhood, I think," he said, his voice not unlike Robby's. He introduced himself and Penny told him her name, leaving off the "Mrs."

"Yes," she added, "I live on the east side of Gramercy Park. Have for about ten years," she smiled prettily.

"Oh, really? I live on the northwest corner, but we're newcomers, only about five years."

"You and your family?"

"No. Well, yes. My son and I. I'm divorced."

"So am I."

"Any children?" He sipped thoughtfully from his glass, his eyes flowing furtively over her sexy body. She looked more like a high-class prostitute than a divorced resident of Gramercy Park, but she spoke like an educated woman, her voice attractive and appealing to him.

From the end of the bar, Bob watched them talk. He felt a twinge of jealousy, and was amazed at how radically Mrs. Luckner had changed in a mere two days. Monday night she'd been six feet deep in her own misery. Today she was floating on clouds, bright and happy and almost too much alive, especially in that scandalous dress.

"Just one boy, eleven years old," Penny answered, adding that this year Jeff was with his father, and that next year he would be with her. Mr. Breining commented on her youthful appearance, not wanting to believe she had a son that old.

"Oh, he's that old all right, and he's got me worried." She thought her lead-in couldn't have been more ideal. Now she knew just what her plan would be.

"Curiously, I'm having a rather serious problem, too," the distinguished gentleman said. "My Robby's got me all muddled today," he said quite seriously, a firmness gripping his mouth. At the sound of her lover's name, Penny felt a vibrant twitching in her pussy.

"Penny, would you care to join me at the table? I mean, if you have a few minutes. Maybe we could help each other...being old parents, I mean," he grinned pleasantly.

"Since we both have young boys, maybe we could at that," she smiled. "Mine's a little bugger. He needs a better father than he's got."

"And when I tell you that my boy is probably worse, I mean it. And what Robby needs is a jail term in Delinquency High."

Penny swished into the darkened booth. She saw the man's quick eyes dart to her bare thighs, lingering there and then looking away politely. Her skirt flared open, and before she closed it demurely, she wondered if he could see her dark nest of pussy hair. She felt his eyes on her firm breasts as she made herself comfortable. He carried both their drinks to the table and sat next to her on the outside. Penny slid on the seat, moving closer to the wall. Her skirt inched up her legs, and her flesh stuck slightly to the vinyl.

Bob shrugged his shoulders. You can never tell, he admitted dryly to himself, shaking his head. Maybe she was a prostitute. Again she shifted in the seat, this time turning to face him. He couldn't help but to look down. The skirt was stretched tight over her upper thighs, her legs slightly spread. He thought he could see the dark, mossy hair between her milky white thighs. Oh God, he moaned to himself, she's not wearing any panties. He had a sudden urge to slip his hand into the dark space between her open legs.

Penny could feel the heat of the man's body close to hers. She promptly took the initiative and spelled out a long but concise story of her son's involvement with an older boy in his school. They had been caught having homosexual relations, she lied, and her son had been the aggressor. That her son had initiated the encounter was most bewildering to her. But, sadly and unjustly, the older lad had been put on

136

report and punished, while her son went free. Her ex-husband had been called to the school. He had been outraged. He had telephoned her only a week ago, soliciting her advice.

She looked up at Robby's father when she finished speaking, her eyes unusually soft, a helpless expression shadowing her face. Inwardly, she was smiling. Her story sounded quite, quite convincing, judging by the interested look in her new friend's dark brown eyes. He definitely had the same eyes as Robby.

"This is such a coincidence," Mr. Breining remarked. "Indeed it is!" His features dissolved into a scowl. Then he softened. "Only last night," he began, and then went on, quite candidly, to report exactly what Robby had told her over the telephone, but adding details that Robby hadn't and exaggerating slightly by saying he had locked the boys in Robby's room.

"But since the incident with my son, I've been doing a lot of reading," said Penny. "I've learned a great deal about sexuality. I even remembered that when I was a young girl I'd several times hugged another naked schoolmate in bed during sleepovers."

Robert F. Breining, Sr. was listening attentively.

"At the time, I felt guilty about it, but now that I'm mature and a mother, I tend to view the whole subject as part of growing up."

"But boys are different," he argued. "Don't you think?"

"Well, I only know my own situation, about Jeff, I mean. I didn't think he should be punished as my ex-husband decided he should be. You know, pulling him out of school and putting him into another for a change of environment, severing his relationships with his close friends, especially the boy my son is said to have literally raped. Imagine a boy of ten raping a boy of twelve?" she laughed.

"You mean it went that far? Sodomy?"

137

"So they say." She felt a little guilty about making up such a horrible lie about her son. It was almost as if she were betraying him.

"Oh, my Lord. I never thought of that! Do you suppose Robby and this Richie are…are doing that?"

Penny looked him right in the eye. "When you were young, probably attending the same academy as your son"—he nodded affirmatively—"did you ever have a homosexual experience, Robert?"

Robert Breining sat back. He put his well-shaped hands on the table. He looked at her once and then turned away from her inquisitive gaze. He looked extremely flustered. He seemed to be considering an answer, then he looked back into her eyes, his lips slightly parted. "I just realized that I did…in fact, several times. Lord help me! I really had forgotten."

Having not thought about it for many years, the memory was at first dim. There had been a boy in college, a fellow crew member, perhaps. God, how easy it was to block certain things from one's memory, he thought, the image now coming more vividly to mind. Of course, it had been a fellow crew member—what was his name? Robert couldn't remember. But he remembered clearly now the details of their relationship.

They'd raced that day; it had been a cool, crisp autumn afternoon. After winning, they'd gone, just the two of them, to the bank of the Charles River, on which they'd earlier rowed, and had shared a bottle of champagne. For a moment, Richard wondered why they'd left the other team members. But then it came to him; something had been stirring between him and what's his name—Stuart, yes that was it! Stuart—for some time. How strange and awful that feeling had been, to desire another man, a teammate. But he had felt it the moment he'd seen Stuart.

He'd been the perfect specimen of masculinity, his physique and beauty matched only by Robert's.

They'd instantly taken a liking to one another, both having clung to feelings of superiority and the resulting alienation from the other team members.

They'd become drinking buddies, going, after each race, to share in the team's victory, which they'd both felt was theirs alone. After perhaps five times of doing this, their relationship had become somewhat more intimate, though not physically so. They'd spoken of girls, of their families, of their feelings that they were destined to greatness. They'd both been overjoyed to finally have someone in whom to confide such things, as they could never have spoken of them to those to whom they favorably compared themselves.

Their looks began to grow warmer, more yearning, so that Stuart had, after a few too many drinks, actually begun to cry in his affection for Robert. Robert, also drunk, had put his arm around him and told him that, to be sure, the feelings were reciprocated. Robert could remember plain as day the look that then came over Stuart's eyes. He remembered it because he had assumed his look was the same.

Then, on that autumn afternoon, they'd gone to the bank of the river, anxious to share in their victory alone, away from the other team members. Afternoon had passed to evening and evening to night, and by nightfall they were both considerably drunk. It had been Stuart who had first reached out to touch Robert. He had touched his thigh, Robert remembered, feeling as he did, a slight stirring in his loins. His hand had lingered there, sliding, after a time, slowly up to Robert's lap. Robert had struggled with the question of stopping him, but had found that he couldn't, that his desire for the boy was too great. As Stuart's hand neared Robert's lap, Robert had felt his cock grow hard. At first, he'd been ashamed, but knowing that this would be their secret, he had taken his hand away from it, exposing his hardness beneath his trousers to his overjoyed friend.

Then they had embraced, falling back on the cold ground, their bodies turning to face one another. They had shifted closer, coming finally to press against each other's bodies, both cocks now hard. Robert had initiated the kiss, moving his mouth over Stuart's, his lips opening to let in Stuart's hungry tongue. They'd kissed for a long time, each boy's tongue exploring the other's mouth, tasting the other's salty moisture.

There had been an overwhelming feeling of guilt, Robert recalled, but it had been overshadowed by Stuart's hand undoing Robert's trousers. There had been nothing he could do to stop his urges. He had had to admit to himself that no matter how hard he might protest, he would continue to want the boy. His cock had sprung hard and big away from his open trousers. Stuart had taken his hand to it, wrapping his fingers around it and squeezing. Robert could still hear the moan that had escaped his throat to the feel of the boy's enclosing fingers. Then he had reached out and placed his palm flat to Stuart's erect cock, which was still covered by his trousers.

Stuart had undressed himself, urging in a throaty whisper, Robert to do the same. Soon, under the iron-grey autumn sky, the stars obscured by clouds, they were both naked, their bodies moving in close together to keep warm. And how warm Stuart's body had been, Robert thought with a renewed stirring sensation in his groin. He could still remember the exquisite feeling of Stuart's soft, young skin pressing on his own. Within minutes of lying there and urging their cocks into the other's belly and thighs, sometimes rubbing them together, they had both come onto one another's flesh.

Robert had lain there afterwards, envisioning eternal hell. But Stuart's mouth closing around his still-hard cock had driven all such thoughts out of his mind. The boy had been expert at bringing him to another orgasm, sucking his cock with alternate vigor and gentleness. He'd come deep in his throat and afterwards, he'd taken Stuart's cock into his mouth and, tasting the peculiar taste of him, had licked the soft, hot flesh of the head of his cock, still somewhat afraid of committing himself fully to the act of sucking another boy's cock. Finally, Stuart, on the verge of coming, his moans certain to signal to any passing stroller the nature of their meaning, had thrust his buttocks off the ground, thus forcing his cock fully into Robert's mouth, who had then taken it willingly in, sliding his firmly gripping lips up and down the hard length of it until Stuart came.

Penny smiled coyly. "Well," she smiled at him, admiring his teeth and his clean-shaven face, "then what's all the excitement?"

He reflected momentarily, then his face brightened. He toasted her with his glass. "I guess it's not half as bad as I thought. After all, nothing drastic happened to me sexually. I've always enjoyed heterosexuality," he grinned. "With pretty girls," he winked, "and I'm not making a play for you, twinkle eyes, even if you are pretty."

"Well, thank you, Mr. Breining."

"You're very welcome, Mrs. ah…?"

"My married name is Luckner."

He looked startled. "You were George Luckner's wife? I wonder why I never met you?"

"I don't. At least during the time I was married to George." Penny asked him about his acquaintance with her ex-husband, and he mentioned that he'd met him at one of the annual meetings of the Gramercy Park Committee, which served as a watchdog of the very exclusive park and the four bordering streets.

He then urged Penny to finish her drink, and he ordered a refill from Bob, who obliged. Penny thought she detected a kind of critical look in old Bob's protective eyes. She smiled up at him when he placed the drinks on the table, wanting to reassure him that she was in safe hands. Bob acknowledged her with a shrug of his shoulders and a smile, which was recognizably subdued.

"You know, Penny," Robert Breining went on, not wanting to leave the subject, "I guess what cured me was my first girlfriend. I mean, probably that was the reason that those brief homosexual encounters, and now I can't even honestly recall the boys' faces, were insignificant to my development. Believe me," he smiled handsomely, "once I had a taste of femininity, I was turned loose like a colt on a prairie. Until, that is, I married Robby's mother. I confess to once thinking that I suffered from excessive sexual desire. I actually worried that I was abnormal. I had so many girls and even an older woman, that after a time I couldn't handle them all. Would you believe that by the time I was married I'd had nearly twenty girls?"

It was not a question that needed an answer, and both took sips from their drinks. Penny felt confident that the pressure he'd been anxious to put on Robby had all but dissolved. She knew he agreed with her that youthful homosexuality was natural for boys, especially those who attended expensive, private, boys-only schools. As he struggled to grow more comfortable with his son's recent activities, he glanced at her firm breasts, which were almost obscenely visible beneath her sweater. Looking up from her drink, she caught his eyes searching, almost caressing, her erect nipples, and he coughed uncomfortably and shut his eyes. When they opened, he was glancing down at the floor. This made her smile.

"You know, Penny, I really appreciate this little conversation we're having today. As a matter of fact, you've enlightened me! I suppose I'll simply have to overlook his shenanigans with Richie and try to get him fixed up with a girl who can understand the problem." He lit her cigarette when she put a fresh one into her silver holder and then his own. "By chance, just by chance, you don't know of any young but wise girls who…who might be interested in, shall we say, training a young man like Robby? You know, getting him interested in girls?"

Without answering him, she went on to commend him for this splendid idea, while inwardly feeling a sharp pang of jealousy. She couldn't bear the thought of her wonderful Robby in the arms of any other female. She mentioned that she'd once read something about a father arranging a meeting between his young son and a prostitute.

"Oh, that would never, never do, Penny. Never! There's the problem of disease, of course, not to mention the possible scandal should the girl in question discover that I was his father. Never!"

Suddenly Penny saw very clearly the possible outcome of this discussion. If his line of thinking advanced far enough, she was certain that he would think of her. The idea of it set her imagination ablaze.

"I would pay the girl generously, and Robby would never have to find out who had set it up," he smiled. "Perhaps I could hire an actress or someone like that. Their meeting could be arranged to appear accidental. She would teach him. He would change his sexual inclinations from boys to girls the way it should be, and I'd have nothing to worry about then…except possibly…" He cut himself off and stared at her. "Penny?"

"Yes? Yes, Robert?" She knew it was going to happen now. He was going to ask her to be the understanding woman. Her emotions welled up inside her and she felt her heart almost stopping. Her cunt grew warm at the thought of Robby.

He shook his head. "No, no," he said, more to himself than to her.

"Excuse me, Robert?"

"Excuse *me*, Penny," he said, his face deadly serious.

She laughed and it sounded to Robert like the merry tinkling of silver bells. "I want another drink, Mr. Breining!" She knew he had almost asked her, and she knew he would eventually. He was obviously trying to summon up his courage, to find a polite and inoffensive way to approach her.

"And so do I, Mrs. Luckner. So do I!" He called Bob, and Bob, no longer amused at the tenor of the conversation at the table, made two new drinks and carried them over, his face as stiff as if he'd been at a funeral.

"Penny…Penny," Robert Breining said, sounding tentative on purpose. It was his belief that he had only to hint at the suggestion and that she would pick it up from there, understanding fully why he was asking her. She did, after all, have a total understanding of the problem. "Oh, no. No. No!"

"You're confusing me, Robert."

"You've thought about it, and you don't know anyone, a pretty girl, say in her twenties or even thirties, intelligent, and understanding of young boys' sexual problems, who would be tender with the boy and explain her body to him?"

"Not a soul."

"Not a soul," he repeated sadly. "You know, it just occurred to me that Robby's pal could use some of the same educational therapy. Perhaps I'll telephone his father, saying nothing of course about Richie's and Robby's involvement. I'll appeal to his sense of tradition and say that it's about time the boys learned something about sex—tell him some story about having learned it myself from someone more experienced than I. He'll probably come up with the name of a young girl whose services we might employ. Does that sound reasonable, Penny?"

"Very reasonable. I think your Robby and this Richie, his friend, would be happy, to say the least. They'd both probably go out of their minds!"

"I guess they might," he smiled. "I wish my old man had done the same for me, that is, what I now really intend to do for my son. Your idea's a brilliant one, young lady."

"I'm not that young, Mr. Breining!"

"Oh, Penny, not *that* young, but you *are* young!"

"I'm thirty. Just!" she laughed. She felt like twenty.

"Well, you certainly don't look it," he exclaimed. "If I'd had to guess your age when you first walked in, I would have doubted the bartender would serve you."

"Seriously, Robert?"

He nodded. "Of course, thirty's a damn sexy age," he said, eyeing the swell of flesh coming out from the neckline of her sweater. "If you don't mind my saying so, your hair spilling down your shoulders like that and your flawless complexion are quite alluring."

"How about my breasts?" she asked, her voice coming out in a whisper. After all, she knew that her breasts were far more alluring than her complexion. He nodded solemnly.

"I know what you mean, Robert, thirty is sexy. But the way you see me now is exactly the way I looked when I was twenty-two."

"Penny," he said, again very serious, keeping to his point, "does twenty-two sound like a good age for this girl we have in mind?"

"Sounds just right, Robert."

"Well, good then. We've reached a scientific decision."

Penny remembered Robby mentioning that he wanted to be a scientist like his father. Cleverly changing the subject, Penny soon had Robby's father telling her about his work in oceanography and marine genetics, in which he'd been deeply and profoundly involved all his adult life. He mentioned that his son shared his interests.

Penny refused another drink, but said she'd keep him company while he enjoyed his. "Does your son and this friend of his have sex...I mean, get together often, Robert?"

"Once is enough for me. I couldn't believe my eyes the way they were going at each other!"

"Not sodomy?"

"No, they were using their mouths."

"You know, Robert, candidly speaking, I see nothing really wrong with that. Women use their mouths on men's genitals—and men on women's—all the time. It's gotten to be very natural, I hear. Not like it used to be even when I was a young girl."

"I guess so," he smiled, remembering her age and quickly estimating that he was just about nineteen years older than she. That wasn't too much of a disadvantage. In fact, Richie's father was remarried to a woman twenty-two years his junior.

They sat silently for a while. She looked up at him. She decided that now seemed to be the perfect time. Now or never, she told herself, feeling a wild shiver spread over her body and three successive spasms inside her pussy.

"Robert, I think it's really going to be difficult to find the right kind of girl. I've been racking my brain while I've been listening to you talk, and I can't think of anyone who would really understand."

His eyes lit up. Maybe if she volunteered, he was thinking, she'd save him a mighty embarrassment.

"It just this moment occurred to me that if everything else were equal, I mean, with absolute discretion, I might be the right woman for the job."

He looked shocked, but she saw through it.

"Oh, never! Never, Penny. That would be impossible. Why, you live right here on the park. We do, too. You could never disguise who you are. That's for sure!"

"What strikes me, Robert, is that in all these years of living right across the park from you and your son, I've not seen you once."

"If you played this part, Penny, and you do agree with me that it's very important, fate would be sure to have you and Robby meet."

"I don't agree. He *is* going away to school soon, isn't he?"

"In about two weeks." He paused. "I was going to send the boy up to Cape Cod for a week before school starts, but a little while ago, after I caught him and Richie, I withdrew the offer."

"You know, that sounds like a good place for this experiment to take place. There are so many young, pretty girls on the Cape, I'm sure that if, by chance, we ever did encounter each other down here in the city, your Robby'd only think that I looked similar to the girl who taught him the facts of life in one of those quaint, isolated cabins on the dunes around Provincetown."

"You're beginning to make me wish I were Robby."

"Yes. Yes, Robert, I think I'm game. And to tell you a secret, the whole idea's beginning to appeal more and more. I have to laugh. Me with a young boy of eighteen, teaching him the function of his penis; me, naked as he examines my body, maybe kissing it. Say," she exclaimed, "wouldn't this be the joke of jokes if he fell in love with lovely, beautiful, older, sexy me?"

They both laughed heartily.

"Penny, I'd pay for everything."

"You mean you think it's a good idea, Robert?"

"Well, if you want to know the truth, I actually think it might work. If anyone can blast these tendencies out of him, it's you. You're ravishing, you know."

"Why, thank you, Robert. You've very kind."

"Penny, listen, if you *are* game and not just teasing

me, I'll be very generous. The boy means more to me than you know!"

"I have enough money, thank you," she smiled, and pressed his hand. "You could take me to dinner when it's all over, however. That would be nice."

Spontaneously, Robert Breining threw his arms around Penny's shoulders and embraced her. "I'm so grateful to you, Penny. Believe me, you'll never know. And I know this adventure will be a success."

"You'll make all the arrangements, then, and let me know?"

"To the last detail," he assured her.

"Very well then, Robert," she said softly, pleased with her campaign, "if you promise to overlook Robby's episode with young Richie and pretend that it never happened, I'll be on your side. I'll even compose a written report!" She laughed happily. "This might be fun!" she exclaimed.

"I envy my son," he said solemnly.

She squeezed his shoulder, pressing her full breasts against his chest, which heaved in his increasingly heavy breathing.

"Maybe I should offer refresher courses to older men, too?" she asked, her voice full of laughter but carrying with it an unmistakable tone of seriousness as well. Her hand slid down his arm. Robert turned his head to see if anyone were looking their way. The bar was empty, their corner dark.

"Might be useful," he said. He slipped his hand between her silky, warm thighs, his fingers coming immediately against her moist, naked flesh. She writhed a little in her seat and put her hand to his cock, which had grown instantly erect at the feel of her cunt. She unzipped his trousers and took his cock into her hands.

"It's like this, see," she said, squeezing his flesh hard. "This is your cock," she was now whispering in his ear so that no one would be able to hear. "And this is my hand." She squeezed again, running it quickly up and down two times. "And this, this is my cunt," she moaned, placing two of his fingers inside herself. "If you spread my lips, you will find a perfect treasure there." She guided his finger to her clitoris. "That's my pleasure," she said when his thumb found it and began to softly rub it. "Now I'll show you *your* pleasure." They laughed softly, and he closed his eyes after taking one final sip from his drink.

Beneath the table, Penny moved her hand to her cunt, wetting her fingers with the moisture from it, and took hold of his cock again. She began to pump her hand up and down, holding him tightly.

"Is this your pleasure?" she asked. He nodded, his eyes still closed. Should Bob have looked over, it would have been plain as anything what they were doing. No one sat in a booth drinking with such a sublime look on his face without either having his cock touched furtively beneath the table. Penny warned him of this and Robert forced his eyes to open. But her hand began to work itself with more pressure and speed up and down his cock, and there was nothing he could do to keep from dropping his lids. His quickly increasing pleasure was too great.

"You haven't answered me. Is this your pleasure?" She rubbed the head of his cock between her forefinger and thumb, pinching slightly, while placing her other hand over his on her cunt and making him rub her clitoris with more speed. He groaned.

"Yes, yes, this is my…" and then she felt his cock expand and throb against her fingers. She could feel the blood pumping hard through the veins, his pleasure being released. She took her own finger to her cunt; in the intensity of his approaching orgasm, he could not move. She rubbed herself vigorously while letting up on the firmness of her grip on his cock. She wanted them to come at the same time. But Robert, who could not contain himself, whose pleasure was right at the surface, ready to explode, grabbed her hand and put it back where it was.

Maybe it was the violence with which he seized her hand, she didn't know, but Penny began to warm exquisitely and to shudder. Her hand, holding his cock, squeezed hard, as hard and as forceful as was her orgasm, which flowed from the tip of her finger to her clitoris and through her body. She could feel his fluids falling onto her wrist, and afterwards, she wiped them off with a napkin while he zipped his trousers back up. Both looked around them to make sure no one had seen. And then they began to laugh, much to Bob's consternation.

They left the bar arm in arm.

Chapter Sixteen

Penny Luckner let herself into her apartment. From the doorway, she saw the sad spectacle of Robby and Richie sitting forlornly on the leather couch, their legs parted and their young bodies hunched over, both suffering the acute miseries of those about to walk to their death.

Four empty beer cans sat on the long coffee table in front of them. The single ashtray was overflowing with half-smoked cigarettes. And, as if to make matters worse and the atmosphere more gloomy, Bach's *Missa Solemnis* was sluggishly approaching its morbid finale.

Since they'd been admitted to the apartment by the doorman they'd argued their case to each other until they were blue in the face, trying to find a rationale Robby's father would accept. Now they were soberly discussing a suicide pact.

Each was quietly itemizing the details of his last will and testament when they heard Penny laugh.

She jumped up on the end of the couch. "Young perverts, you cocksuckers, bad, bad boys, filthy-minded creatures, hearken and listen to me!"

"She's gone batty!" Richie observed.

"Looks like it," Robby concurred.

Penny plopped down on the couch like a young kid and roared with laughter. They both stared at her as if she'd suffered a violent nervous breakdown.

But her joyful laughter reached them, and soon neither could resist a smile.

"I came, I saw your father, Robby, and I conquered him!" she exclaimed, standing up again on the couch and folding her arms like General Patton...or was it Mussolini? She couldn't remember.

"You saw him?" Robby asked eagerly, sitting up.

"Relax, boys," she grinned. "You're both home safe, thanks to little Penny here."

"You mean that? Even me?" Richie asked, his voice squeaking.

"Yes, you little cocksucker!" she laughed again. She felt absolutely ecstatic! What a grand play she'd pulled!

"If one of you perverts will make Penny about two fingers worth of scotch with lots of ice cubes, she will give you both a full report on the engagement with the enemy at Pete's Tavern.

They both rushed to the kitchen, and she doubled over, still laughing. Tears filled her eyes as the image of the two of them sitting so forsakenly on the couch passed before her again and again. Oh, these kids! She wiped her eyes, but each time she tried to be serious, the wild mood would sweep over her and she'd begin giggling.

In the kitchen, she heard Richie say, "I really think she's lost her marbles, Robby."

"I admit she's a little scary," was the answer.

"She's freaking out!"

"And so am I," Robby said soberly.

"Come in here, you two!" Penny yelled. "Right now!"

It took her fifteen minutes to relate the story to them, and when she was finished, they both fell over her, tearing her clothes from her body and showering her with kisses and repeated words of gratitude. When she was naked, she stepped away from their encircling arms, walking across the room. When she reached the window, she stood there for some moments, her back to them, her nakedness to the world.

Turning around slowly, she said, "Now, we've got to be very careful about how we proceed." Then she began to walk stealthily toward them, her breasts swaying slightly from side to side, her thighs tensing and relaxing in her walk.

"I can hardly believe it's true," said Robby. Penny could see tears of relief well up in his eyes. She took him into her arms, pulling him to her nakedness, and wiped the tears away with her softly brushing lips. Then she hugged his face to her breasts, and he began to sob freely and shiver so that she held him tighter to her warmth.

"Didn't I tell you I'd solve the problem?" she asked softly, petting his hair.

"But it wasn't solvable," Robby sobbed, clutching her warm nakedness close to him, his fingernails scratching her flesh, his lips kissing her breasts, gently tugging on her nipples between words. "I don't understand how you did it. He's such a bastard." He bit down on her nipple hard as if to punctuate his feelings for his father.

"I found him to be a real gentleman. He's actually very understanding. I didn't have to persuade him at all. In fact, he persuaded me." She had the sense that Robby was mindlessly saying things that would give her cause to hold him closer to her body. She felt his lips brushing along the deep valley where her breasts converged, his nose buried there, his warm breath on her flesh.

Gently, she pushed him away. "Now let's drink to our good fortune. And then, Robby, I think you should call your father. Tell him that you and Richie have discussed things and that you'll both come there for dinner. Tell him that you'd like advice on sex. He'll tell you about the plan, but he won't spell it out for you. He'll just tell you that you're going to the Cape. But you have to be careful not to give him any indication that you know what's to happen. That would ruin all of us."

"Don't worry, I can handle it," he said, staring at her statuesque body before him. He could feel his cock growing hard at the very sight of her.

"What about me?" asked Richie, his voice sounding child-like. "He won't tell my father?"

153

Penny could see that Richie's fears had not abated. "No. I told you, Robby's father has put the whole thing out of his mind. It never happened."

Richie looked skeptical, but allowed himself to be pulled into Penny's embrace by her outreaching arms. She hugged him to the side of her body while pulling Robby back in as well. She rocked them both as if they were children.

"I think we should celebrate," her breath came out warm on the top of Robby's head as she was kissing him when she spoke. "But first, Robby, call your father."

Robby went to the phone reluctantly, frightened that his father had somehow tricked Penny into believing that he was kinder than he really was. In the meantime, Penny fixed three drinks. When she was carrying them back to the living room, Robby was returning from the phone call, his face beaming.

"Seems you were right," he said, taking the glass from Penny's hand. "I can't believe it." He took a sip, his eyes searching Penny's body as he swallowed the cool liquid. "He's taking us to dinner in Chelsea," he said to Richie who looked a bit more relieved.

"See? It's all fixed up. Now, we have about two hours to have some fun together. Take off your clothes, both of you." Penny grinned into her glass as she watched the boys immediately begin to undress. Richie did so deliberately, as if his lingering skepticism slowed his reactions, and Robby did so eagerly, his cock bursting free of his trousers as soon as he'd unzipped them.

When they were fully naked, she gripped their naked pricks and led them to her bedroom. Their pricks began to harden in her hand. She had to smile, looking at their angelic faces, their youthful shoulders and boyish bottoms. She had fallen in love with their bodies—which were sleek and masculine without being fully adult—their smooth skin, and their thickening growth of pubic hair from which their clean, young pricks seemed to grow like sturdy saplings. She felt a weird compassion for other women her age, whose lives were probably devoid of the passion and excitement she was now experiencing.

"Come. Lie down, both of you, and show Penny exactly what you both were doing when the old monster walked in."

She wanted to see them touching each other, sucking each other, but she'd also decided that this would be the last time. She had become certain that they'd needed this sort of activity between them only as a boyish reaching out for sexual knowledge. She was sure they could be convinced, indeed convince themselves, that with a healthy, sexually vibrant woman between them to share, her delicious body readily available to them, they would require little else to satisfy themselves.

She was sure she'd made the proper decision and that her thinking was neither stiffly moral nor illogical. She was amused at her clinical approach as she heard them laugh when she pulled down the coverlet and bared the white sheets.

She sat down in a chair near the bed and watched as Robby climbed atop Richie's supine body. His legs spread to let Robby in. She could see Robby pushing his hardened cock between Richie's thighs and Richie squeeze them together. For a moment, Robby pushed himself in and out of the tight space as if he were fucking the boy; Richie's cock was pressed hard to his belly. They kissed deeply, their tongues twisting around each other. Penny could see their saliva glistening on their chins. Then Robby turned his body around, lowered his head and slipped his lips over Richie's enflamed cock. When he did, Richie caught Robby's cock in his mouth and began immediately to suck on it.

"Both of you, suck harder." She took her hands to her breasts, cupping them and pushing them together. Her fingers squeezed her nipples, causing them to stand out from her white flesh like rosy buds of flowers. "Does it feel good?" Her cunt ached, and she longed to be in the center of them, both of their tongues sweeping over her sex, entering her. She watched their slow response: both boys nodded without letting up on their rhythmic sucking.

"Do it faster," she said, beginning to finger her clitoris. She stared in complete and utter arousal at the two heads bobbing on the slippery cocks. She had a better view of Robby's mouth enclosed around Richie's cock. She watched as it disappeared inside Robby's mouth and then reappeared, wetted with his saliva. When Robby bore down on the cock, taking it fully into his mouth, his lips folded into the movement so that for a moment he appeared lipless. And then, letting the cock slowly slip from his mouth, his lips reappeared; full and red and glistening. Richie began to pump himself to the rhythm of his increased passion.

"Suck on each other's balls," she ordered. She saw Robby pull his cock from Richie's mouth, his buttocks rising like the moon into the air, and his balls spreading out over Richie's wetted face. Richie squirmed, and Robby dipped his tongue into the dark space between Richie's thighs, lightly tickling his soft balls. Penny raised her legs and balanced her feet on the edge of the chair. She let her knees fall open and cupped her pussy with her palm, rubbing her clitoris with her thumb. The heat from her hand warmed her cunt and sent tremors through her body.

And then, unable to bear the agonizing torture of having his cock so close to Richie's mouth, Robby thrust it back in, Richie's teeth scraping the soft flesh. He moaned. Robby took Richie's cock back into his mouth at the same time. Their pumping became frantic, speaking to their increased desire. Penny circled her fingers around her clitoris, all the while staring at the reddened flesh of Richie's cock moving in and out of her lover's mouth. For a moment, she watched Richie's balls rubbing his thighs.

She reached beneath her and fingered her asshole, pushing just the tip of her finger into it. She loved the sight of Robby's buttocks expanding and contracting as he drove in and out of Richie's mouth. It looked truly as if he were fucking a woman.

Penny climbed onto the bed and crouched behind Richie's head, her breasts hanging pendulant over his brow. Leaning over, she licked Robby's asshole, causing him to moan deeply and bear down harder against Richie's firm gripping lips. Her tongue darted out again, jabbing into Robby's asshole, and she saw his full buttocks clench tightly, his cock burying itself in Richie's mouth, the tip of it touching the boy's expanding throat. Again, she jabbed her tongue at his ass, and again he thrust hard into Richie's now straining mouth, all the while keeping a tight hold on Richie's cock. She pushed her firm tongue into Robby's asshole, and he came, shuddering, feeling the warm filling sensation in his ass and the soft envelopment of Richie's mouth.

Richie, feeling his friend's throbbing cock against his tongue, jerked his buttocks upwards, thus driving his own cock into the back of Robby's throat. He, too, came then, each boy exploding into the other's mouth. Afterwards, Penny lay back naked, her arms and legs splayed, and asked them to lick her all over.

She opened her arms, and Robby fell into them. He kissed her breasts, his lips falling into the space between them, his cheeks rubbing to the sides of them. She felt Richie's less agile movements parting her legs. His head was between her thighs, his tongue wetting the flesh there. She felt the top of his head brushing against the surface of her cunt, and she spread her legs wider apart.

"Richie wants to go to the moon with you, Penny," whispered Robby. "But he's nervous because he's never sucked a woman's cunt before." Robby's voice was tender and soft, and Penny felt as if she would burst with love for him. She reached down and held her hand to Richie's mouth. He parted his lips and licked between her fingers, taking each one into his mouth and sucking it. Then she guided him to her cunt by moving her hand there, his lips still wrapped around one of her fingers.

"Don't be nervous, Richie. It'll seem natural to you, as if you were born to please me, once you taste me, feel me with your tongue." As soon as the last word escaped her mouth, she felt the tip of his searching tongue come out to lick her outer folds. She moaned to encourage him, and he began to part her folds forcefully, with broad, lapping strokes. Robby lowered his head back to her breasts. Penny swooned inwardly to the feel of Robby's mouth closing around her nipple and Richie's tongue gently exploring the intricacies of her sex. Warmth crept over her body, already bathed in the late afternoon sun.

She began to feel drowsy. She wanted a sip of scotch but was too lazy and too comfortable to sit up and reach for her glass. She breathed deeply, Richie's swirling tongue now leaping gallantly and knowingly inside her fiery pussy. She squirmed and writhed languorously as Robby sucked her breasts into his mouth, his one hand down close to Richie's face, tickling her clitoris while his friend sucked and licked her nectar-sweet pussy.

"Oh, life, you're so good to me," she sighed aloud. Robby hugged her tighter and kissed her lips. She opened her mouth and sucked his tongue into it, biting it with her teeth; then she plunged her own tongue back into his mouth, squirming it around his teeth and the inside walls of his cheeks. She began to writhe on the bed, rotating and gyrating her hips as Richie sucked and drank in the rich cream seeping from her slit and coating his worshipping tongue.

She was thinking she could go on like this forever when suddenly, abruptly as a thunderclap, the ear-splitting, piercing, noise of the telephone made her leap off the bed!

"Holy shit!" she swore.

"It's only the phone," said Richie looking up, his face smeared with her juices.

She had to smile. He looked so cute and innocent and the expression in his clouded eyes was very funny to her. "Oh, I know," she said, "but I was having such a marvelous time." She sat up and slipped off the bed with some effort. I'll be back in a few seconds. Don't either of you go away."

Chapter Seventeen

When Penny returned from the telephone, she saw Robby and Richie sucking each other's pricks. This time Richie was on top, his firm buttocks clenched tight as his cock drove deep into Robby's mouth. Robby's legs were parted and bent as he thrust upwards into the boy's throat. They were unmindful of her return, their hands gripping each other's hips and thighs, their bodies working in perfect rhythm.

She watched this idyllic scene for a moment or so. Then she entered her bedroom and stretched out on the bed on her stomach, her exquisitely molded buttocks, so milky white and silky, now raised slightly as she slipped a pillow under her lower belly. She spread her legs apart and began to rotate her hips on the pillow, grinding her hot crotch against the cool material.

"That was your father, Robby. We have nothing to worry about now, absolutely nothing. And Richie, that includes you, because Robby's dad has talked with your father. He said nothing at all about his catching you blowing each other, but only mentioned only his idea about Robby and the girl he'd met in Provincetown who would teach him all he would need to know about fucking," she laughed merrily as she winked at both of them.

"So," she continued, "Richie's father knows a girl in Provincetown who will cooperate, and I'll betcha she's not as pretty or as sexy as me, and Richie'll go with her; you, Robby, will be with me."

She asked them to fondle and play with her buttocks and her asshole while she explained the balance of the phone conversation with Robert F. Breining.

As she spoke, she reached over to her bedside table and withdrew from it a bottle of cream.

Handing it to Robby, she told him to generously anoint her asshole with it. Feeling the cold cream touching her hole, she squirmed a little on the bed and then settled back into place when she felt Robby's warm fingers begin to work it into her flesh. Richie's hands spread her buttocks apart, his fingers sinking into them. Then she began to describe the conversation with Robby's father, feeling all the while the exquisite sensations of Robby's palm rubbing the cream into her ass, his finger dipping into her hole.

"Well, kids, this is what's going to happen: Tomorrow at noon, both of you are flying up to Boston. From there you'll fly to the Cape, and go across the bay on an inter-island plane. From there you'll fly in a seaplane to your father's experimental station where you'll spend the night, because he couldn't get reservations until the day after tomorrow. When you get up you'll fly back again to Provincetown and check into the Black Dog Inn, where a room will be waiting for the two of you. How does that sound?"

As the boy's excitement increased, they began to play more roughly with her. They began to slap her buttocks, spanking her playfully, to spread her ass cheeks wide, licking along the deep crevice between them; they thrust their fists between her thighs, their knuckles rubbing her cunt. Someone's finger entered her cunt while another's slipped well-lubricated into her asshole. She moaned. This is what she had wanted for so long.

The spanking continued. They slapped her buttocks hard, causing her white flesh to redden. They hit first the soft, full flesh of them before moving down to spank the backs of her thighs and continuing on down to her calves. Someone's lips were taking in her toes, a tongue swirling around them while the other boy continued to spank her.

"Yes, lick my toes and my feet," she moaned, raising her feet in the air, parting her knees wider. She rubbed her pussy against the fluffy pillow, enjoying the pressure on her clitoris.

Penny's face was buried in the crook of her arm. Her eyes were closed. She had no idea which young man was doing what to her vibrating body, but she could feel hands and fingers fluttering all over her. A tongue flashed across her wiggling toes; a warm, wet mouth sucked on her big toe; and then a finger—or was it two?—slipped into her pouting asshole. She felt more fingers marauding inside her cunt and one searching for her burning clitoris.

Nothing could be more wonderful than two delightfully naked young men making love to her steaming body, she thought, when suddenly she felt the pressure of something much larger than a fingertip against the opening of her gasping asshole. She knew it must be a prick. Secretly, she hoped it was Robby. She wanted her youthful lover to take her anal virginity, and she was dying to feel his thick, long, hot prick explode between her buttocks. As she lay there now, she was amazed at how often she had dreamed about this.

Peeking, she saw it was him. She closed her eyes and spoke only once, saying, "Whoever it is who's going to fuck me up my ass, don't worry about hurting me, and if I yell out, for Christ's sake don't take out your prick, okay?"

She felt two affirmative slaps, one on either naked buttock, and clamping her eyes shut, she reached down with one hand to grip her clitoris and waited for the marvelous prick to enter and begin fucking her asshole.

There was no threat of interruption this time. She'd taken the phone off the hook.

Robby, on his knees behind her upturned buttocks, guided the head of his hot prick and rubbed it all over the small opening, lubricating the velvet tip of his tool before nudging it gently into the darkness, which at first seemed to refuse him entry.

He adjusted his position several times until it was just right. "You help me spread her cheeks," Robby whispered to Richie, who'd been cupping Robby's hanging balls as he stared in fascination at the size of the head of his friend's prick and the tiny hole it was expected to penetrate.

Richie sat closer. With both hands, he stretched her ass cheeks wide apart. Now her asshole was totally visible, pouting open just slightly as the tip of Robby's prick nosed against it.

Penny groaned when Robby gave a little shove. His prick was beginning to slide into her asshole. She moved her hips gently, raising herself off the pillow so that her buttocks pushed against his prick, the backs of her thighs rubbing to Robby's. Then she moved her thighs closer together, and his prick slid in a whole two inches. Penny screamed. It felt so hot; it wasn't at all like the handle of the knife sharpener. Why? Then she realized it must be the curve of Robby's prick. The handle was straight.

Robby was patient for a moment, just kneeling and listening to Penny whimper. He moved gently, his prick inching further into her ass now, feeling the tightness of her narrow channel. When she began gyrating her hips again, asking for more, Robby pressed against her with a series of little jabs which forced his prick up another inch, and then another. He could hardly believe that it was truly burying itself up her tight asshole.

Penny was now moaning steadily and writhing her naked bottom, loving the fullness she was feeling up her asshole. She could feel his prick pulsating. She began to rock her body gently, her fingers now pulling on her burning clitoris. She could sense Robby's tension; she knew that he wanted to fuck her hard, but that he was being patient, understanding somehow that she wanted to get used to the large prick before it was shoved it all the way up to the hilt.

Then he pushed, holding onto her narrow waist, gripping her flesh and pulling his body toward her buttocks, his prick penetrating to the root.

"Oh, my God! It feels like it's the size of your arm, but don't pull it out! I love it! Oh, Robby, I love it up there. It's so hot and thick, I can feel the pretty head of it. It's deep in my ass. Oh, Robby, darling, I love your prick! Oh, Robby, fuck me now. Yes, darling, fuck me up my ass. Yes. That's it! Just like up my hot cunt, darling. Move it out a little bit, and then push it back in. Move it out more and shove it all the way back into my asshole. Now fuck me harder. Use my asshole, Robby. Fuck it. Fuck my ass! Slap my cheeks! Richie, while you watch Robby's prick moving up my ass, slap my buttocks hard! Make them all red. Bright red! Make them sting with your hands, Richie…while Robby shoves his precious prick in and out!" She couldn't speak anymore, the last of her words having come out as moans rather than actual speech.

Robby began to pump rhythmically in and out of her while Richie struck her ass hard with the palm of his hand. His eyes stayed glued to Robby's shining, hard prick as it plowed into Penny and pulled out, still glistening, still hard. He watched as Robby's balls slapped against Penny's thighs, coming in gentle contact with her enlarged clitoris. Penny moaned deeply each time he thrust his cock into her. She writhed when he pulled it out. Her fingers were buried in her cunt, her thumb rubbing her clitoris.

She fucked back violently on his cock, grinding her hips against his own, her buttocks slamming against his hard belly. The contrast between him thrusting deep into her and withdrawing, her buttock muscles forcing him out, excited her wildly, causing her to almost faint. It was both excruciatingly painful and exquisitely pleasurable at once. And added to this was the sharp, stinging pain of Richie's blows to her buttocks and the sideways glance she caught of him playing with himself, his fingers curling around his cock and tugging at it. It was all too much for her, and yet she never wanted it to end.

Penny looked around. "Slow down, darling," she said. "I can't take any more. It's getting so hot in there your prick is boiling hot!"

Slowly, Penny let her muscles squeeze his prick out of her dark, hot asshole. It was magnificently erect and glistening from the grease he'd used and his own seminal discharges. He almost came twice but was able each time to strain and hold back the powerful feeling that was about to envelop him. He sat back on his haunches, looking down at her crimson bottom, which was still stinging from Richie's fierce spanking.

Penny rolled over and sat up. Both boys went immediately to her and began to suck on her damp breasts. Penny held their heads, her eyes closed, her asshole burning and her emotions still at fever pitch. She felt their lapping tongues glide across her tingling nipples, licking all of her smooth, full flesh, flowing into her armpits and then back to her breasts. With their noses, they lifted her heavy breasts, their brows weighted by the soft undersides. Then dropping them they began to nibble and bite on her nipples.

Listening to the grandfather clock strike the quarter hour, Penny's heart fluttered. They would have to leave soon. "Quickly," she said, "Robby, get on your back now and spread your legs. I'm going to lie on top of you, and you put your prick into my cunt, okay?" She kissed Richie on the lips, holding his cheeks. "You, Richie, get into the same position you saw Robby in when he was fucking my asshole, and you get your prick in there like Robby did. Then," she sighed, her face brightening, "I'll have two wonderful cocks in me at the very same time…"

"That's possible?" Richie asked, bewildered. He thought he'd jerked off thinking about every possible position, but he'd never thought of this one.

She climbed atop Robby and lowered herself on his uprising cock. The folds of her cunt closed around him softly, yet firmly. The pleasure of having him fully within her was immense. Now she wanted the pain. She reached behind her and led Richie's cock to her hole, telling him to spread her ass cheeks while she guided it in. He did, his nails digging into her skin. The head slipped in, and she pushed back on it.

"That's right, Richie. Take it easy and it will slide in. That's right. A little more…oh, yes, lots more…lots more, right now. Do it now, Richie! Give me your cock! Oh, two pricks at once! Oh, oh, two…two hot pricks at once, one up my ass…oh, up my ass…and the other…the other…the other…Oh, fuck me…fuck me. Both of you, fuck me! Oh, Richie! Richie, fuck it deep, that's…that's how…oh, Robby, buck up like that, yes, deeper, scratch me, yes…suck on my breasts…suck on my nipples, yes, bite them. Bite them! Oh, Richie, push…push…push…Fuck my ass! Fuck my cunt! I'm going insane!"

They worked their cocks into her alternately, so that when Richie thrust deeply into her, Robby pulled out. Then as Richie withdrew, Robby drove in. He plunged in as far as he could go. He kept himself there, held firmly and warmly by the walls of her gripping cunt. Then, in one ecstatic instant, he felt the tip of Richie's prick pounding against his own; Richie was buried now deeply in her ass. For a moment, both boys remained like that, feeling their cocks rubbing through the thin wall that separated them. Penny felt as if she were being torn apart.

Her clitoris rubbed at the base of Robby's cock, Richie's balls pressing against the convergence of their bodies. She writhed against both boys, their cocks circling slowly inside of her. She squeezed the muscles in her ass and cunt tightly and felt the first onrushing waves of her orgasm. She began to sob unearthly cries as she pounded on Robby's cock, rising and falling madly, as if possessed.

She lurched so violently on Robby's prick that the thrust of her buttocks caught poor Richie unprepared, and he was knocked completely off the bed onto the rug, his eyes wide with surprise and his prick still throbbing as though it were still buried in her sucking asshole.

"Oh," Penny wailed, "how beautiful. How beautiful."

She rolled off Robby, and then, her eyes hazy but still functioning, she noticed Robby's prick looming up like a mast from his belly. She fell on it with her mouth and sucked it ferociously. She reached for Richie, and he came up and snuggled next to Robby, his own prick now in Penny's hand while she sucked violently on Robby's powerful tool.

"Come…come…Robby! Come! Shoot off into my mouth, darling," she screamed, licking and chewing and jerking his prick and tickling and squeezing his balls, all at the same time. "Shoot off into my mouth. Oh, Robby, I want to drink your come, darling. Shoot! Shoot, come, come into my mouth!" She licked him frantically and took his entire length down her throat.

These words, hot, dirty and stimulating, proved to be more effective on Richie than Robby. His cock in Penny's hand began to leap and throb. Richie was going to come! She knew it. She quickly raised her mouth from Robby's prick and plunged down on Richie's just in time, for he exploded that split second, his come jetting into her mouth, slamming

168

against the inside of her cheeks, blasting against her tongue and shooting down her throat as she plunged her head up and down wildly. Her eyes closed and then opened, her fingers squeezing his balls and her other hand jerking the shaft so as to wring every last drop from it.

She lay with her face pressing against Richie's pulsating prick, her tongue licking it and her lips kissing it tenderly. Then she raised up and looked down at Robby.

"What's the matter, darling?" He looked so sad. "Tell me what's bothering you."

"I couldn't come. I just couldn't come, Penny. I don't know what's wrong. But I got so close to it, and then I couldn't come. Something's wrong. I'm sure there is. Because I can come in Richie's mouth with no trouble at all. Right, Richie?"

Richie nodded. "Lot's of come, too," he added helpfully.

With a sudden rush of fear, Robby understood perfectly well what would make him come; when he'd been fucking Penny in the ass, he'd imagined that it was Richie who he was fucking. The look that came over his face in the realization of this imparted his knowledge to Penny. Both glanced at an unknowing Richie. Penny, though infinitely disappointed, told Richie to lay prone on the bed. Despite her promise to Robby's father, she wanted him to feel the powerful pleasure which was now waning in her body.

Richie, not quite understanding what was happening, felt the cool cream being spread over his ass. He squirmed in sudden understanding, trying to get away from the probing fingers. Sure, he'd liked having his cock sucked by Robby. He'd even liked doing it more than he could describe. But to be fucked in his ass by him? That was perhaps more than he wanted. But Penny's hands held him firm to the bed. He

169

felt the head of Robby's enraged cock pushing against his hole, sliding along the crevice, touching his balls.

And then, with a shout of extreme pleasure, Robby thrust into him, his cock buried in one instant deep in Richie's ass. The pain was greater than Richie ever would have imagined; Robby's pleasure was intense. His cock expanded and throbbed in the tight passageway. He could hardly contain himself.

"This feels so good," he murmured. Richie's cock, despite the pain, grew hard beneath him. There was something strangely pleasurable about it; filling, warm. As his cock grew harder, the realization that he was being fucked in the ass by another man became easier to accept. There wasn't anything wrong with it, he told himself. In fact, it felt very good. He felt the length of Robby's strong thighs pressing against the backs of his, Robbie's chest heavy on his back, Robby's hot breath on his neck. He could hear the deep-throated moans settling in his ear. He rubbed his cock against the bed beneath him, but the bed yielded too easily, so he moved his hand to grasp his cock while raising his buttocks into the air.

Just as his fingers gripped his cock, the feeling of Robby's cock seeming to fill him, he felt the first spasm of his release. He felt Robby's cock throbbing to the walls of his ass. He squeezed himself hard, and it was as if he were releasing warmth from his cock to his body. Robby bore down hard and came, his veins pounding within Richie's inner walls, his fluids shooting into his ass. Richie rubbed his cock hard. He, too, came, wetting the sheets beneath him. It was horrible and good at once, and afterwards he looked into his friend's sublime eyes imploringly.

"It's okay, Richie," said Robby, leaning over to kiss him full on the mouth. "There's nothing wrong with it. I love your ass, your cock. It felt so good to have my cock buried in you like that, better than any-thing." Both boys hugged, and Penny realized that her assurances to Robby's father had been false. Robby would not give up men for women. He would always, she thought, enjoy both.

When the clock struck the hour, Penny managed to get the boys dressed and scurry them out and on their way across Gramercy Park to Robby's father. Penny, after the telephone call, now trusted him implicitly to be understanding and wise in his treat-ment of the problem. She was glad he had not wit-nessed Robby's latest foray into homosexuality.

Penny took a long bath, and then, after napping for several hours—a time of exceedingly pleasant erotic dreams—she awakened.

Naked, she walked into the living room. She glanced at the grandfather clock and saw that it was close to nine. She smiled, rubbing her hands over her ripe breasts. She pinched her nipples and then reached behind her to feel her asshole. She smiled again and ran her finger up and down the crevice, sticking the tip into it quickly, and the memory of the two exquisite pricks fucking her sent shivers through her body.

Deciding that she'd dress and keep her usual noc-turnal appointment at Pete's Tavern, she left the apartment promptly at ten.

On the sidewalk, she circled the perimeter of the park, and then, using her key, she entered the north gate, crossing through the center of the strikingly green oasis. She saw squirrels leaping and cavorting, an old man sitting alone and drawing on his pipe, a forgotten bicycle and a striped beach ball. She stopped by the caretaker's cabin and entered. It was just as they'd left it the night before. She sighed deeply as she let the scene of debauchery float across her mind. She licked her lips, recalling the boys play-ing with each other's rigid pricks while she smeared her pussy juices all over her naked breasts, licking her fingers as they sat on the floor staring up at her.

She went out of the cabin and closed the door. She passed the statue of Washington Irving and then walked to the exit gate at the south end.

She couldn't remember being happier. Walking along, her long hair bouncing on her shoulders, her lovely, voluptuous breasts swaying sensually, she went through the door into Pete's Tavern.

She sat at the bar. The bartender was new. She ordered her drink and inserted a cigarette into her silver holder.

From behind, she felt a light tap on her shoulder. She turned. Her eyes widened and her lips parted in complete surprise.

"Good evening, Mrs. Luckner. I had hoped that you would come. I've been sort of waiting for you."

"Good evening to you, Mr. Breining," Penny sighed, having to catch her breath.

He held out his hands. "Would you join me, Penny?"

Her bright eyes were beaming into his. "Yes. Yes, I would. I would."

They went to the same booth they'd sat in earlier that day. Discussing the finer points of their plan, they were both secretly perusing the contours of the other's body with their furtive eyes. After a few drinks, their pursuits became less furtive and more obvious so that it became necessary to address them. Penny reached her hand across the seat to touch his leg. She inched it up slowly, saying that she was sure he had a fine son, and that their plan would be a success.

She touched his cock, which hardened against her palm, and again took it out of his pants. He grunted and shifted closer to her. She brought him to a quick orgasm, the bar more crowded now than it had been in the afternoon; her movements were quicker and more forceful because of it. Her breasts ached against her sweater, but he could not touch them. With his sperm dripping from the underside of the table, he slipped his hand between her thighs. He encountered her moist cunt, and he stuck two fingers into her. She moaned and spread her legs wide. He pushed his fingers deeper in and pulled them out.

"This is how I would fuck you," he said, his voice hoarse with desire, his fingers moving slowly in and out. She circled her finger around her clitoris and imagined that his hand was his cock.

"I'd like you to fuck me," she whispered, her finger working with increased speed around the center of her sex. He inserted two more fingers so that he had four buried within her.

"I'd move slowly at first," he said, "like this, reveling in the softness of your cunt. Then I'd increase in speed until I was pounding into you." His fingers moved faster now, wetted by the moistness of her desire, and she rubbed her clitoris until she came, her body shuddering, her eyes closing tightly. "That'll be part of the plan," he said afterwards, withdrawing his fingers and taking them to his mouth. Licking them, uncaring suddenly if any one saw, he looked into her eyes. "First you'll teach my son, and then when you return you'll teach me." Secretly, Penny feared that his son had already been taught; he'd learned that afternoon what gave him the greatest pleasure. She said nothing though and finished her drink.

At Robby's house, the two boys were sleeping that night in separate bedrooms, so as not to give further cause for Robby's father to be angry with them. Alone in bed, both boys lay awake, their cocks hard in their separate memories of the afternoon, and in anticipation of their trip.

Richie imagined Penny, her soft flesh, her large breasts and enveloping cunt. He touched himself. His hands became her cunt, squeezing him, bringing his pleasure to the surface. He pumped himself with increased vigor as her cunt became her mouth and her mouth her ass. And then all faded into one, becoming a great, enveloping chasm of womanness, and he exploded into his fist.

Robby, in the other room, was tormented. His cock, which rose into the air, ached and yet he would not touch it; he couldn't touch himself when all he could imagine was fucking Richie. He was full of guilt, despite his words of encouragement to Richie, and felt that if he brought himself to orgasm by imagining fucking the boy, he would be doomed for life. And yet, he was in pain, his cock throbbing in the air, screaming to be touched.

He tossed onto his side and tried to think of other things. But still he thought of Richie, his guilt overwhelming him. He turned onto his stomach and pressed his hardened cock into the bed. Richie's ass had been so tight, his cock so hard beneath him as he'd fucked him. He had enjoyed it too! What was wrong with him? Why had be been able to take pleasure in Penny before and then, with Richie there, suddenly unable to? He didn't understand, and he continued to rub his cock against the soft cotton sheets. What was happening to him?

Imagining that Richie was just in the next room, probably touching himself, Robby reached his hand beneath him and grasped his cock, unmindful suddenly of his guilt. He didn't care! It felt too good wrapping his fingers around himself, squeezing. So what if he wanted to fuck Richie a thousand times? So what? He squeezed and slipped his hand tight down the length of himself, still pressed against the bed. The head slipped out of the top of his fist, and he turned onto his back. So what?

He sucked on his finger, wetting it, and ran it around the head of his cock. It felt so good. He bore down on the base and thought of being buried deep within Richie's ass. And then, in a flood of pleasure, it came to him. He squeezed himself hard, pumping up and down; he wanted Richie to fuck him in the ass. The thought of it was like a velvet cloak enclosing him. He imagined Richie kneeling behind him, his hands on his hips; he imagined him driving into him; he imagined the feel of the boy's hard cock held fully inside of him. Thinking this, he came in a series of blinding spasms, his come shooting onto his stomach, his hand gripping himself firmly. His orgasm seemed endless, and all thought was reduced to one thing: Richie kneeling behind him and driving his cock into his ass.

When his pleasure waned, he tossed again on the bed, overcome with a greater sense of guilt and fear than ever before. What was happening? He fell into dreamless sleep and awoke in the morning with an erection. His first thought was of Richie.

Two nights later, they were all safely on the Cape. Robby and Penny were lying naked together in bed. They were talking, and Robby was idly caressing her belly, fondling her breasts.

"I don't understand," he said. "I was so overwhelmed with your body, why can't I be anymore? What's happened? It's not like I can't get an erection just looking at you, because I can. I just can't seem to have an orgasm."

"It's all right, darling," said Penny, her hand lingering over his soft penis. "These things happen. It's not to say that you won't ever desire another woman again. Maybe you're just in the throes of discovery now. Maybe when it all settles in, when you become used to the bounty of pleasure around you, you'll get your old self back. You really shouldn't worry so much about it, that just makes it worse."

She rolled away from him and sat at his feet. Spreading her legs, she leaned against the board at the foot of the bed.

"Just watch," she said, "just watch me." Her cunt was pink and red and flower-like as it opened to the touch of her finger. He stared at it and at the rhythmic movement of her wrist and hand. Her breasts swayed slightly with her breathing. He could see her clitoris rising red and hard away from her folds. His cock grew hard.

"Don't touch yourself," she instructed. She moved her hand to her breast while still circling a finger around her clitoris. Within minutes, Robby could see her cunt begin to pulse and expand to her desire.

"I'm coming now," she whispered. She began to heave her buttocks off the bed, her breasts now swaying more frantically from side to side. Her legs were spread wide, so that they lay against the bed. Her cunt grew deeper in color and began to open and close violently. Robby's cock burned to be touched, but he resisted. And then, her orgasm fully upon her, he saw her creamy liquids coming out from her hole. He wanted to lick them, to drink from her. He moved to her.

When he was between her legs she pulled him up her body and he entered her, thrusting deep into her. The passage was smooth and silky and warm. It had been such agony sitting there with his cock pounding to be touched that the instant in which it was fully enveloped within her he was flooded with passion and pleasure and he came, groaning to be deeper within her than was possible. His body jerked on top of hers, and she held him tightly to her by pressing her hands into his buttocks. When his body stilled she kissed him on the lips and laughed.

"See?" she said. "You've nothing at all to worry about."

Robby smiled, but still he knew that he wanted Richie more than her; still he longed to by fucked by Richie, like he'd just fucked her. It was horrible, and yet the promise of the possibility of it was sweeter than anything he'd ever known before.

Elsewhere, Richie and his new friend were getting acquainted, ostensibly to teach him for the first time about sex. She was pressing her breasts to his thrusting cock. His buttocks clenched, and he slid deep into the valley of her breasts and came onto her chin. With her finger, she wiped it away and then licked her finger.

"Do you think you'll be ready for my cunt soon?" she asked. Richie nodded. He wondered what Robby and Penny were doing at that moment. He missed them and didn't like this woman very much. She was coarse and cold, though willing to let him do anything with her body that he desired.

"Yeah, probably, just let me sleep for awhile. I'm tired for some reason." She rolled to the side and lit a cigarette.

"Sure," she said, "sure." Robby slept five hours, dreaming all the while about Penny and Robby. It was unfair, he thought, that he was the one left out. He awoke to a soft mouth enveloping his cock. Without opening his eyes he assumed it was his new friend. He would come into her mouth, and then they would eat dinner, he thought. He had no doubts that he would come soon; it didn't matter how cold and coarse she was, she was still a woman and he still wanted to fuck her a thousand times.

Opening his eyes, he looked down his body and saw not the woman, but Robby. It was Robby sucking his cock! A wild tremor shot through his body, and he thrust his hips upwards in renewed desire. Penny was sitting at the edge of the bed.

"We came to find you because poor Robby couldn't do without you." Richie smiled, happy to be back with his real friends.

"Where's the woman?" he asked, his eyes closing in a sudden surge of warm pleasure as Robby's tongue spiraled up his cock.

"We sent her away. I gave her some money to be

177

sure she'd give a good report on you." Again
Richie laughed, and his fingers gripped the sheets
at his sides, his knuckles white, his buttocks rising
off the bed. His cock vanished into Robby's mouth,
the tip of it touching his throat. Robby snorted as
he drank the flow of hot fluid. It tasted delicious to
him, and he couldn't wait until later, when he would
feel it between his thighs, wetting his cock and
balls. Finally Robby lifted his head to look at his
friend. He licked his lips languidly, reveling in the
taste of the sperm, and told him how glad he was to
see him.

Penny, seeing the happiness in the two boys'
faces, felt for the first time since she'd met Robby,
lonely again. It seemed suddenly that they didn't
even remember her, that they were happy enough
to be together. It occurred to her that upon her
return to the city she might not see them again. But
then Richie turned to look at her, and she moved
onto his body, taking Robby down with her. The
three of them lay there, indiscriminately touching
one another. Robby's and Richie's education now
complete, they both kissed Penny on the mouth to
thank her. All three mouths opened to the others,
their tongues playfully entwined.

There was nothing new left to learn; now they
had only to learn how to enjoy more fully, without
youthful urgency, those things that gave them the
greatest pleasure. Robby kneeled behind Richie,
who continued to kiss Penny, and drove into him,
his fingers parting his buttocks with painful force.
Robby moaned deeply and said something about
feeling no guilt. Penny grasped Richie's cock and
led it to her cunt. She felt him being pushed and
pulled by the strength of Robby's violent passion
for him. Richie moved little on his own, instead
allowing himself to be manipulated by Robby driving into him and pulling out. Thus did Richie move

within Penny's cunt, wondering what felt better: her cunt or Robby's cock. Without coming to any decision, he sat back in order to take Robby more deeply in, his cock pulling away from Penny's yearning hold.

Other Books Available From
MASQUERADE'S
EROTIC LIBRARY

THE TEARS OF THE INQUISITION   34-3 $4.95

"Even now, in mortal terror, Rosanna's nakedness reminded her of her happily married nights. There was a tickling inside her as her nervous system reminded her that she was ready for sex. But before her was a man for whom she could feel only the most deeply rooted horror—the Inquisitor!"

POOR DARLINGS   33-5 $4.95

Here are the impressions and feelings, the excitement and lust, that young women feel when they submit to desire. Not just with male partners—but with women too. Desperate, gasping, scandalous sex!

THE LUSTFUL TURK   28-9 $4.95

In 1814, Emily Bartow's ship was captured by Tunisian pirates. The innocent young bride, just entering the bloom of womanhood, was picked to be held for ransom—but held in the harem of the Dey of Tunis, where she was sexually broken in by crazed eunuchs, corrupted by lesbian slave girls, and then given to the queen as a sexual toy. Turkish lust unleashed!

MARCUS VAN HELLER

ADAM & EVE   93-9 $4.95

A young couple, Adam and Eve, long to escape their dull lives by achieving stardom—she in the theater, and he in the art scene. They're willing to do anything to become successful, including trading their luscious bodies for a big break. Eve soon finds herself acting cozy on the casting couch, while Adam must join a bizarre sex cult to further his artistic career. Corruption is the price paid for fame in this electrifying tale of ambition and desire!

KIDNAP   90-4 $4.95

Nick Harding is called in to investigate a mysterious kidnapping case involving the rich and powerful in London, France and Geneva. Along the way he has the pleasure of "interrogating" a sensuous exotic dancer named Jeanne and a beautiful English reporter, as he finds himself further enmeshed in the sleazy international crime underworld. A sizzling mystery of sexual intrigue and betrayal!

THE MASQUERADE READERS

DOUBLE NOVEL   86-6 $6.95

Two bestselling novels of illicit desire, combined into one spellbinding volume! Paul Little's *The Metamorphosis of Lisette Joyaux* tells the story of an innocent young woman seduced by a group of beautiful and experienced lesbians who initiate her into a new world of pleasure. *The Story of Monique* explores an underground society's clandestine rituals and scandalous encounters that beckon to the ripe and willing Monique.

A MASQUERADE READER   84-X $4.95

Masquerade presents a salacious selection of excerpts from its library of erotica. Infamously strict lessons are learned at the hand of *The English Governess* and *Nina Foxton*, where the notorious Nina proves herself a very harsh taskmistress. Scandalous confessions are to be found in the *Diary of an Angel*, and the harrowing story of a woman whose desires drove her to the ultimate sacrifice in *Thongs* completes this collection. Leaves you hungry for more!

ROBERT DESMOND

PROFESSIONAL CHARMER   3003-2 $4.95
A dissolute gigolo lives a parasitical life of luxury by providing his sexual services to the rich and bored. Traveling in the most exclusive social circles, this gun-for-hire will gratify the lewdest and most vulgar cravings for nothing more than a fine meal or a shred of stylish clothing. Each and every exploit he must perform is described in lurid detail, in this story of a prostitute's progress!

THE SWEETEST FRUIT   95-5 $4.95
A twisted tale of revenge and seduction! Connie Lashfield is determined to seduce and destroy pious Father Chadcroft to show her former lover, Ben Trawler, that she no longer requires his sexual services. She corrupts the priest into forsaking all that he holds sacred, destroys his peaceful parish, and slyly manipulates him with her smouldering looks and hypnotic sexual aura. But little does she know that he's followed her lecherous lead—and taken a saucy lover of his own!

MICHAEL DRAX

OBSESSIONS   3012-1 $4.95
Gorgeous, haughty Victoria is determined to become a top model, using her special abilities to sexually ensnare the powerful men and women who control the fashion industry: Michael, the rich voyeur, who enjoys photographing Victoria almost as much as she enjoys taunting and teasing him. Paige, reunited with Victoria after a long-ago night of anonymous passion,who finds herself compelled to witness Victoria's conquests. Pietro and Alex, who take turns and then join in for a sizzling threesome. All are obsessed with Victoria—but only one is the object of her unquenchable desire!

SARA ADAMSON

THE CATALYST   3015-6 $4.95
The forbidden world of SM is explored in this story of initiation and discovery. After viewing a controversial, explicitly kinky film full of images of bondage and submission, several audience members find themselves deeply moved by the erotic suggestions they've seen on the screen. A lesbian couple spank and make up after a heated argument. Two gay men pick up a leatherman to help them re-enact their favorite scenes from the film. A suburban married couple break out the rope and engage in a drama of surrender and control. These are just a few of the first-time experiments set off by *THE CATALYST!*

THE CLASSIC COLLECTION

MAN WITH A MAID: The Conclusion   3013-X $4.95
The final chapter in the classic saga of lust and domination that has thrilled readers for decades. Jack and his willful wife Alice seek out new prey to suffer the pleasures and delights of the Snuggery. The adulterous sister who is corrected with enthusiasm, and the clumsy maid who receives a grueling hour of guidance, are just two of the damsels who benefit from the lessons learned under the lash and paddle!

THE YELLOW ROOM 96-3 $4.95

Two complete erotic masterpieces. The "yellow room" holds the secrets of lust, lechery and the lash. There, bare-bottomed, spread-eagled and open to the world, demure Alice Darvell soon learns to love her lickings from her perverted guardian. Even more exciting is the second torrid tale of hot heiress Rosa Coote and her adventures in punishment and pleasure with her two sexy, sadistic servants, Jane and Jemima. Feverishly erotic!

THE BOUDOIR 85-8 $4.95

Masquerade presents a new edition of the classic Victorian magazine, including several bawdy novellas, ribald stories, and indecent anecdotes to arouse and delight. Six volumes of this original journal of indiscretion are presented here in all their salacious glory. Good old-fashioned smut!

A WEEKEND VISIT 59-9 $4.95

"Dear Jack, Can you come down for a long weekend visit and amuse three lonely females? I am writing at mother's suggestion. Do come!" Fresh from his erotic exploits in *Man with a Maid*, randy Jack is at it again!

THE ENGLISH GOVERNESS 43-2 $4.95

When Lord Lovell's son was expelled from his prep school for masturbation, his father hired a governess to tutor the motherless boy—giving her strict instructions not to spare the rod to break him of his bad habits. But governess Harriet Marwood was addicted to domination. The whip was her loving instrument. With it, she taught young Richard Lovell to use the rod in ways he had never dreamed possible. The downward path to perversion!

PLEASURES AND FOLLIES 26-2 $4.95

The Erotikon of an English libertine: "I got astride her, rode her roughshod, plied the crop....Ashamed by these excesses provoked by my reading, I compiled a well-seasoned Erotikon and it excited me to such a degree that I...well, pick up my book, gentle reader, and you'll see whether it has a similar effect upon you."

STUDENTS OF PASSION 22-X $4.95

When she arrives at the prestigious Beauchamp Academy, Francine is young, innocent, and eager to learn. But her daily lessons have nothing to do with grammar and spelling. Her teachers and schoolmates enroll her in a course devoted to passion, anatomy, and lust...and she's determine to graduate with honors.

SACRED PASSIONS 21-1 $4.95

Young Augustus comes into the heavenly sanctuary, seeking protection from the enemies of his debt-ridden father. Soon he discovers that the joys of the body far surpass those of the spirit.

THE NUNNERY TALES 20-3 $4.95

Innocent novices are helpless in the hands of corrupt clerics. The Abbess forces her rites of sexual initiation on any maiden who falls into her hands. Father Abelard delivers his penance with smart strokes of the whip on his female penitents' bottoms. After exposure to the Mother Superior and her lustful nuns, sweet Emilie, Louise, and the other novices are sexual novices no longer. Cloistered concubinage!

MAN WITH A MAID 15-7 $4.95

The ultimate epic of sexual domination. In the Snuggery, a padded, soundproofed room equipped with wall pulleys, a strap-down table, and a chair with hand and leg shackles, untiring pervert Jack bends beautiful Alice to his will. She not only gives in to his lewd desire; she becomes more lascivious than he, and corrupts her maid and her best friend into lesbianism Perhaps the hottest book

FRUITS OF PASSION 05-X $4.95

A classic study of Victorian sexual obsession. From his initiation into end-less orgiastic delights by the slippery lips of the chambermaid sisters, Rose and Manette, the Count de Leon continues his erotic diary for forty years, ending with his Caribbean voyages with the two most uninhibited Victorian Venuses he has ever known. A life totally dedicated to sex!

ALEXANDER TROCCHI

WHITE THIGHS 3009-1 $4.95

A dark fantasy of sexual obsession from a modern erotic master, Alexander Trocchi. This is the story of young Saul and his sexual fixation on beautiful, tormented Anna of the white thighs. Their scorching, dangerous passion leads to murder and madness every time they submit. Saul must possess her again and again, no matter what or who stands in his way. A powerful and disturbing masterpiece!

SCHOOL FOR SIN . 89-0 $4.95

When Peggy Flynn leaves the harsh morality of her Irish country home behind for the bright lights of Dublin, her sensuous nature leads to her seduction by a handsome and mysterious stranger. He recruits her into a training school with an uncommon curriculum. Together with the other students, she embarks on an unusual education in erotic pleasures. No one knows what awaits them at gradu-ation, but each student is sure to be well-schooled in sex!

MY LIFE AND LOVES (THE 'LOST' VOLUME) 52-1 $4.95

What happens when you try to fake a sequel to the most scandalous autobi-ography of the 20th century? If the "forger" is one of the most important figures in modern Erotica, you get a masterpiece, and *this is it!*

THONGS 46-7 $4.95

"Spain, perhaps more than any other country in the world, is the land of passion and of death. And in Spain life is cheap, from that glittering tragedy in the bull-ring to the quick thrust of the stiletto in a narrow street in a Barcelona slum. No, this death would not have called for further comment had it not been for one striking fact. The naked woman had met her end in a way he had never seen before—a way that had enormous sexual significance. My God, she had been..."

THE CARNAL DAYS OF HELEN SEFERIS 35-1 $4.95

Private Investigator Anthony Harvest takes on his greatest challenge. He is determined to find and save Helen Seferis, a beautiful Australian who has been abducted in Algiers. Following clues in Helen's diary, he flies to North Africa and descends into the depths of the white-slave trade. Through exotic slave markets, forbidden harems, and sadistic rites he pursues Helen Seferis, the ultimate sexual prize!

CLASSIC EROTIC BIOGRAPHIES

THE STORY OF MONIQUE 42-4 $4.95

Lovely, innocent Monique found her aunt's friends strange, curious, inviting. There were seven lesbians who came to Aunt Sonia's parties. And a convent nearby where nuns and monks whipped themselves into a frenzy and then fell upon each other in orgiastic madness. Monique became the mistress of *all* their ceremonies; and discovered within herself an endless appetite for sex—the more perverted, the better.!

THE FURTHER ADV. OF MADELEINE   04-1 $4.95

"What mortal pen can describe these driven orgasmic transports," writes Madeleine as she explores Paris' sexual underground. She discovers that the finest clothes may cover the most twisted personalities of all—especially the that of mad monk Grigory Rasputin, whose sexual drives match even Madeleine's. History-making sex!

THE MASQUERADE AMERICAN COLLECTION

DANCE HALL GIRLS   44-0 $4.95

The dance hall studio in Modesto was a ruthless trap for women of all ages. They learned to dance under the tutelage of sexual professionals. So grateful were they for the attention, they opened their hearts and their wallets. Scandalous sexual slavery!

LUSTY LESSONS   31-9 $4.95

David Elston had everything; good breeding, money, a secure job with a promising future, and a beautiful wife—everything except the ability to fulfill the unrelenting demands of his passion. His efforts to satisfy his desires end in failure...until he meets a voluptuous stranger who takes him in hand and leads him to the forbidden land of unattainable pleasure.

THE GILDED LILY   25-4 $4.95

Lily Caldron, struggling actress, knows what she wants—pleasure, passion, and new experiences. But more than that, she wants her big break—one that will launch her career in the movies. She looks for it at Hollywood's most private party, where nothing is forbidden and the only rule is sexual excess. There she meets one of Tinseltown's hottest directors, and becomes submerged in a world of secrets and perversions she never imagined.

JOCELYN JOYCE

THE WILD HEART   3007-5 $4.95

A luxurious hotel in the French Alps is setting for this artful web of sex, desire, and love. A newlywed wife sees sex as a conjugal duty, while her hungry husband tries to awaken her. A ripe Parisian entertains the wealthy guests for the love of money. A swinging couple introduce some new ideas into the marriage of two guests. A delicious variation on the old Inn-and-out!

PRIVATE LIVES   91-2 $4.95

The wealthy French suburb of Dampierre is the setting for this racy soap opera of non-stop action! The illicit affairs and lecherous habits of Dampierre's most illustrious citizens make for a sizzling tale of French erotic life. The wealthy widow who has a craving for a young busboy, who is sleeping with a rich businessman's wife, whose husband is minding his sex business elsewhere, are just a few of Dampierre's randy residents. An unrestrained look at the more sophisticated side of French life!

DEMON HEAT   79-3 $4.95

An ancient vampire stalks the unsuspecting in the form of a beautiful woman. Unlike the legendary Dracula, this fiend doesn't drink blood; she craves a different kind of potion. When her insatiable appetite has drained every last drop of juice from her victims, she leaves them spent and hungering for more—even if it means being sucked to death!

HAREM SONG   73-4 $4.95

Young Amber flees her cruel uncle and provincial English village in search of a better life, but finds she is no match for the streets of London. Amber becomes a classy call girl and is eventually sold into a lusty Sultan's harem—a vocation for which she possesses more than average talent!

JADE EAST   60-2 $4.95

Laura, passive and passionate, follows her domineering husband Emilio to Hong Kong. He gives her to Wu Li, a Chinese connoisseur of sexual perversions, who passes her on to Madeleine, a flamboyant lesbian. Madeleine's friends make Laura the centerpiece in Hong Kong's underground orgies. As she is being taken by three men while the guests watch, Laura sees Emilio with a beautiful, dark-haired girl: he is about to start another on her downward path. A journey into sexual slavery!

RAWHIDE LUST   55-6 $4.95

Diana Beaumont, the young wife of a U.S. Marshal, is kidnapped as an act of vengeance against her husband. Jack Beaumont sets out on a long journey to get his wife back, but finally catches up with her trail only to learn that she's been sold into Mexico. A story of the Old West, when the only law was made by the gun, and a woman's virtue was often worth no more than the price of a few steers!

THE JAZZ AGE   48-3 $4.95

This is an erotic novel of life in the Roaring Twenties. A Wall Street attorney becomes suspicious of his mistress while his wife has an interlude with a lesbian lover. *The Jazz Age* is a romp of erotic realism in the heyday of the flapper and the speakeasy.

LUSCIDIA WALLACE

THE ICE MAIDEN   3001-6 $4.95

Edward Canton has ruthlessly seized everything he wants in life, with one exception: Rebecca Esterbrook. Frustrated by his inability to seduce her with money, he kidnaps her and whisks her away to his remote island compound, where she learns to shed her inhibitions and accept caresses from both men and women. Fully aroused for the first time in her life, she becomes her writhing, red-hot love slave!

KATY'S AWAKENING   74-2 $4.95

Poor Katy thinks she's been rescued by a kindly young couple after a terrible car wreck. Little does she suspect that she's been ensnared by a ring of swingers whose tastes run to domination and wild sex parties. Katy becomes the newest initiate into this private club, and learns the rules from every player!

ALIZARIN LAKE

THE INSTRUMENTS OF THE PASSION   3010-5 $4.95

All that remains is the diary of a young initiate, detailing the twisted rituals of a mysterious cult institution known only as "Rossiter". Behind these sinister walls, a beautiful young woman performs an unending drama of pain and humiliation. What is the impulse that justifies her, night after night, to consent to this strange ceremony? And to what lengths will her aberrant passion drive her?

CLARA   80-7 $4.95

The mysterious death of a beautiful, aristocratic woman leads her old boyfriend on a harrowing journey of discovery. His search uncovers a woman on a quest for deeper and more unusual sensations, each more shocking than the one before!

TUTORED IN LUST   78-5 $4.95

This tale of the initiation and instruction of a carnal college co-ed and her fellow students unlocks the sex secrets of the classroom. Books take a back seat to secret societies and their bizarre ceremonies, in this story of students with an unquenchable thirst for knowledge!

DIARY OF AN ANGEL   71-8 $4.95

A long-forgotten diary tells the story of angelic Victoria, lured into a secret life of unimaginable depravity. "I am like a fly caught in a spider's web, a helpless and voiceless victim of their every whim." This intelligent and shocking novel is destined to become an underground classic.

FESTIVAL OF VENUS   37-8 $4.95

Brigeen Mooney fled her home in the west of Ireland to avoid being forced into a nunnery. But her refuge in Dublin turned out to be dedicated to a different religion. The young women she met there belonged to the Old Religion, devoted to sex and sacrifices. They were competing to become sexual priestesses on the Isle of Man. The sexual ceremonies of pagan gods!

CHINA BLUE

SECRETS OF THE CITY   03-3 $4.75

Her beautiful daughters, fifteen-year-old Eurasian twins, have been abducted by Thai pirates and sold into white slavery. China Blue, the infamous Madame of Saigon, a black belt enchantress in the martial arts of love, is out for revenge. Her search brings her to Manhattan, where she intends to call upon her secret sexual arts to kill her enemies at the height of ecstasy. A sex war!

MARY LOVE

MASTERING MARY SUE   3005-9 $4.95

Mary Sue is a rich nymphomaniac whose husband is determined to pervert her, declare her mentally incompetent, and gain control of her fortune. He brings her to a castle in Europe, where a sadistic psychiatrist and his well-trained servants amuse themselves. To Mary Sue's delight, they have stumbled on an unimaginably depraved sex cult, where panting men and women suffer beneath cruel instructors and every kind of corruption is practiced!

WANDA   3002-4 $4.95

Wanda just can't help it. Ever since she moved to Greenwich Village, she's been overwhelmed by the desire to be totally, utterly naked! By day, she finds herself inspired by a pornographic novel whose main character's insatiable appetites seem to match her own. At night she parades her quivering, nubile flesh in a non-stop sex show for her neighbors. An electrifying exhibitionist gone wild!

ANGELA   76-9 $4.95

A lonely bartender in a Parisian café thinks he's run every con in the book, until a mysterious comes in the cold and changes his mind. Angela's game is "look but don't touch," and she drives everyone crazy with desire, dancing and writhing for their viewing pleasure but never allowing a single caress. Soon her sensual spell is cast, and she's the only one who can break it!

THE EDITORS OF PLAYGIRL

MORE PLAYGIRL FANTASIES   69-6 $4.95

The editors of *Playgirl* bring you more of their favorites from the "Readers' Fantasy Forum." This collection is even hotter than the last, as the readers of *Playgirl* share their most intimate and imaginative fantasy encounters, revealing every steamy detail—daydreams only *Playgirl* readers could pen!

LOUISE BELHAVEL

FRAGRANT ABUSES   88-2 $4.95
The sex saga of Clara and Iris continues as the now-experienced girls enjoy themselves with a new circle of worldly friends whose imaginations definitely match their own. Against an exotic array of locations, Clara and Iris sample the unique delights of every country and its culture!

DEPRAVED ANGELS   92-0 $4.95
The third and final installment in the incredible adventures of Clara and Iris. Together with their friends, lovers, and worldly acquaintances, Clara and Iris explore the frontiers of depravity at home and abroad. Their scandalous sexcapades delight and intrigue everyone, and their natural curiosity and sweet, sexy personalities guarantee that there will always be new and exotic thrills for them to experience just over the next horizon!

TITIAN BERESFORD

JUDITH BOSTON   87-4 $4.95
Young Edward would have been lucky to get the stodgy old companion he thought his parents had hired for him. Instead, an exqusite woman arrives at his door, and from the top of her tightly-wound bun to the tips of her impossibly high heels, Judith Boston is in complete control. Edward finds his compulsively lewd behavior never goes unpunished by the unflinchingly severe Judith Boston!

NINA FOXTON   71-8 $4.95
A young aristocrat finds herself bored by the run-of-the-mill amusements for ladies of good breeding. Instead of taking tea with gentlemen, outrageous Nina invents a device to "milk" them of their most private essences. No one says "No" to Nina!

SINCERITY JONES

SEDUCTIONS   83-1 $4.95
Twelve short stories of erotic encounters, told with a woman's sensibility. This original collection includes couplings of every variety, including a woman who helps fulfill her man's fantasy of making it with another man, a dangerous liaison in the back of a taxi, a uncommon alliance between a Wall Street type and a funky, downtown woman, and a walk on the wild side for a vacationing sexual adventurer. Thoroughly modern women!

PALMIRO VICARION

LUST   82-3 $4.95
A wealthy and powerful man of leisure recounts his rise up the corporate ladder and his corresponding descent into debauchery. Adventure and political intrigue provide a stimulating backdrop for this tale of a classic scoundrel with an uncurbed appetite for sexual power!

PETER JASON

WAYWARD   3004-0 $4.95
A mysterious countess hires a bus and tour guide for an unusual vacation. Traveling through Europe's most notorious cities and resorts, the bus picks up the countess' friends, lovers, and acquaintances from every walk of life. The common thread between these strangers is their libertine philosophy and pursuit of unbridled sensual pleasure. Each guest brings unique sexual tastes and talents to the group, climaxing in countless orgies, outrageous acts, and endless deviation!

A Complete Listing Of
MASQUERADE'S
EROTIC LIBRARY

ORDERING IS EASY!

MC/VISA ORDERS CAN BE PLACED BY CALLING OUR TOLL-FREE NUMBER

1-800-458-9640

OR MAIL THE COUPON BELOW TO:
MASQUERADE BOOKS
801 SECOND AVE.,
NEW YORK, N.Y. 10017

VPP 008-3

QTY	TITLE	NO.	PRICE
	SUBTOTAL		
	POSTAGE and HANDLING		
	TOTAL		

Add $1.00 Postage and Handling for first book and 50¢ for each additional book.
Outside the U.S. add $2.00 for first book, $1.00 for each additional book. New York
State residents add $8^1/4\%$ sales tax.

NAME _____

ADDRESS _____ **APT #** _____

CITY _____ **STATE** _____ **ZIP** _____

TEL ( ) _____

PAYMENT: ☐ CHECK ☐ MONEY ORDER ☐ VISA ☐ MC

CARD NO. _____ **EXP. DATE** _____

PLEASE ALLOW **4-6 WEEKS** DELIVERY. NO C.O.D. ORDERS. PLEASE MAKE ALL
CHECKS PAYABLE TO MASQUERADE BOOKS. PAYABLE IN U.S. CURRENCY ONLY.